Reluctantly Romanced

The Barrington Billionaires

Book Ten

Ruth Cardello

Author Contact
website: RuthCardello.com
email: ruthcardello@gmail.com
Facebook: Author Ruth Cardello
Twitter: RuthieCardello
Goodreads
goodreads.com/author/show/4820876.Ruth_Cardello
Bookbub
bookbub.com/authors/ruth-cardello

New York Times and *USA Today* bestselling author Ruth Cardello returns with a hilarious addition to the Barrington Billionaire series.

Copyright

Print Edition

ISBN eBook: 978-1-951888-08-4
ISBN Print: 978-1-951888-09-1

An original work of Ruth Cardello, 2021.

Dedication

To Aly, who is not a gynecologist, but is every bit as feisty as the character she inspired.

I am so grateful for the strong women in my life.

Chapter One

DYLAN SUTTON CRINGED inwardly when his brother said, "So then I asked, 'Why isn't saying a woman has a vagina of steel a thing?'" He understood how the long transatlantic flight was bringing out the clown in Connor, but also that the humor of the story would be lost on some of the passengers on Clay Landon's private jet.

A quick glance to the side confirmed that one in particular was shaking her beautiful head while pretending to be reading on her tablet. When she looked up, he looked away. If he could have stopped the train wreck that was underway, he would have, but Clay was already laughing and that was all the encouragement Connor needed.

Connor continued, "And Dylan said it would be a puss—" He stopped and looked around before deciding to censor his language. "Anyway, his theory is that steel didn't sound fuckable."

Dylan didn't need to wonder who loudly expelled a breath in disgust. It wasn't his brother's fiancée. She was rolling her eyes, but smiling. It wasn't Claire, the woman who had invested a year into training both Connor and

Dylan how to behave in public. She didn't appear to have heard it. Her prolonged level of distraction was concerning to Dylan, but his guess was it was due to her husband, Ian Barrington, flying over to meet them on his own. Whatever he and Bradford were into, the general consensus was that it was better to not know. They both worked for the government in a capacity no one discussed. Enough said.

Dylan and Connor had grown up in a small town in Upstate New York, raised by a hardworking father who had brought them into their family's construction company as soon as they could hold a hammer. They were driving large machinery while still stretching to reach the pedals and fixing them long before they could legally operate them. Theirs had been a reasonably normal childhood until their sister, Viviana, had married into one of the richest families in the United States and everyone's life had changed.

Trying to fit in had been tricky at first. It had taken a blunt reality check from Clay to smooth the bumpy transition out. He had taken Dylan and Connor aside and explained to them that they drank too much, laughed too loud, and broke too many social rules. If they didn't want to be a constant embarrassment to their sister as well as the butt of everyone's jokes, they would need to make some changes.

Although it hadn't been easy to hear, Clay had been right. Some might have taken such harsh words as an attack, but that hadn't been his intention. He'd followed up the talk not only with a suggestion that the brothers work with Claire but also an introduction to movie producers.

Without Clay's intervention, the lead roles in *Danger*

Doubled would never have been offered to Dylan and Connor. The brothers wouldn't have known what it was like to be catapulted into stardom from the popularity of that movie and Dylan wouldn't have become painfully aware of how inappropriate some private conversations could sound when shared publicly.

He and Connor might not be Barringtons, but they'd become part of the family and there was a responsibility that came with that. If the Barringtons, as well as Clay, were not so welcoming and supportive, Dylan might have resented the changes he'd made for them. He didn't; they'd freed him. Claire had guided them through everything from how to eat at a formal event to the art of saying less rather than more. He was now not only welcomed, but invited to elite gatherings around the globe and could mingle seamlessly—unless his brother was there.

Connor's fiancée, Angelina, smacked her hand on Connor's thigh. "Stop, you're embarrassing Dylan."

Connor shook his head. "Impossible." He looked down at her, his smile widening. "And even if I am, he deserves it. Have you forgotten the motivational boxers he sent me? It took you to explain to me that they were innuendos."

"Of course they were," Aly muttered in a low voice.

Unable to keep the comment to himself, Dylan responded, "Keep reading that romance of yours, no one expects you to have a sense of humor."

She lowered her tablet and shot Dylan a glare. "For your information, I'm reading a study in the Blandet Medical Journal regarding the role of microbiome in recurrent pregnancy loss."

Dammit. No man could have a comeback for that without sounding like an ass. Dylan sat back, folded his arms over his chest, and did what he'd been taught to do—he kept his mouth shut.

As if sensing the sudden tension, Clay's wife clapped her hands together and said, "Two hours until we land. I absolutely love Iceland. It'll be exciting to show you around. And although I was lucky enough to visit the set of *Danger Doubled*, I'm excited to see Dylan in action." Her smile was genuine and coaxing. "Dylan, do you really do all of your own stunts?"

Dylan turned his attention to Lexi with relief. "Most of them. There are some that require skills I don't yet have, but I'm always learning."

"Angelina, Connor has already started filming his next project as well, hasn't he?" Lexi asked.

"Yes, the beginning is set in England, but the rest of it will film in Vermont so we won't have to be apart as much." She rested her head on Connor's shoulder. "I've missed him."

Connor kissed the top of her head. "I missed you too. This trip couldn't have come at a better time. I have a break between filming and we get to see Dylan. I hope the house has a gym. My producer said I don't have to remain as buff as I am, but I can't let Dylan out-muscle me."

"As if I'd ever rent a house without a gym." A smile pulled at Dylan's lips. "Not my fault you chose the role of a doctor last time and now one as a lovesick veterinarian." He flexed his ample bicep for humor. "You don't need these to cure a kitten, but I'm out there blowing up shit and saving the world so I have to look the part."

He told himself not to, but he glanced over to see Aly's reaction. She didn't lift her eyes from her tablet. He shrugged and lowered his arm. Although it was a shame, it might be time for Dylan to concede that his future sister-in-law's friends would never like him. He frowned. Not all of them. Just one. "Hey, has anyone heard from Joanna and Bradford? Are they meeting us at the lodge?"

Clay answered, "That's the understanding. Ian said they are in the air already."

Claire turned away from the window. "Ian will meet us at the house as well. He texted that he's not far behind us."

She looked worried enough that Dylan moved over to sit in the empty seat beside her. Rather than ask about Ian, he chose a topic he hoped would distract her from her concerns. "Is this your first trip to Iceland?"

After a pause, she smiled. "It is. Thank you for inviting us."

Dylan joked, "It feels odd accepting any gratitude for this trip, considering we're flying over in Clay's jet and after I finish reshooting a few scenes we're moving on to the private island Clay arranged."

Clay waved a hand in dismissal of Dylan's words. "Why have a jet if not to use it? And the mainland lodge you chose sounds charming. I only had to make a few tiny enhancements to it."

Lexi interjected, "Clay, I was in charge of setting everything up. Don't you trust Dylan and me?"

With a straight face, Clay said, "The lodge didn't have staff."

Dylan chuckled. "You make that sound like we'd be roughing it."

Not looking at all bothered, Clay asked, "Did you want to be the one cooking breakfast for all of us, Dylan?" With an arched eyebrow he challenged his wife. "Or cleaning up after the ten of us, Lexi?"

Lexi laughed, "Lord, no. Add all the staff you want, babe."

Clay nodded. "I'm always wrong until people realize how right I am."

Still seeking to cheer Claire, Dylan said, "That should be my life's motto."

She shot him a faint smile. "It would be better than some you might have chosen in the past."

Dylan had learned early that playing the clown was an effective way to lighten someone's mood. His mother had been very ill for a long time when he was young, but his antics with Connor had never failed to make her laugh. "So I shouldn't tell you how talking about a steel vagina led Connor and me to stop at this all-you-can-eat seafood place where we literally ate so much lobster they threatened to have us removed if we ordered another plate?" He referenced his height. "Hey, they should have known we could pack food away."

Claire cocked her head to one side. "Okay, now I'm curious. How do you get from vaginas to lobster?"

In unison, Connor and Dylan said, "Swedish meatballs."

"Vaginas of steel." Dylan held up his fingers and referenced the size of an inch. "Balls of steel. Balls. Meatballs. Swedish meatballs. The topic made us hungry. But seriously, they were about to toss us out before someone recognized us. Then they couldn't feed us enough." He touched his stomach. "Lobsters are a lot of work for very little meat, but we did our best to eat ourselves sick, didn't we, Connor?"

"We sure did," his brother said with a chuckle.

"I can picture it so clearly." Claire laughed so hard she wiped tears from her eyes. *She needed that—to just let out some tension.* When she stopped, she touched Dylan's hand lightly. "Thank you."

"You're welcome." Dylan smiled down at her then turned and caught Aly watching him. She wasn't laughing along or even smiling. He shrugged and returned his attention to Claire. "I'm surprised you're not lecturing us on our choice of topics."

Claire shook her head as she said, "No lectures necessary. Every suggestion I gave you was for your public persona. Here with friends, we'd always rather you be you."

You be you.

Dylan nodded even as her words echoed through him. He was very much still a work in progress. There was the beer-drinking, bar-fighting, construction-loving man he'd been before the Barringtons had come into his life. There was the serious big-screen actor he'd become. If someone asked him who he was, he would be hard-pressed to answer them. Was it possible to be two people? His brother brought out one side, time away from Connor and his family allowed him to explore the other one.

No one who met him away from Connor called him a *meathead*.

No one who had known him his whole life would believe he could attend a public event without embarrassing himself.

He glanced over at Aly again. It didn't require a PhD to guess which side she thought was the real him. They'd been thrown together at several events. He'd tried being nice to her. He'd tried flirting with her. He'd even tried ignoring her. Her disdain for him remained the same.

She was a beautiful woman. Intelligent. A gynecologist known for moving the field forward via technology and focused research. If she ever stopped glaring at him, he might tell her how admirable he thought her dedication to her field was. All he wanted was for them to find common ground, some semblance of a friendship that would make things more comfortable when they were all together—for Connor as well as for Angelina.

Aly looked up from her tablet. For just a second he thought he saw something in her eyes besides irritation, a spark of interest, but it was fleeting and he dismissed it as imagined.

While holding Aly's gaze, Dylan answered Claire, "That's good, because all I'll ever be is me."

Aly looked away and Dylan sighed.

It's going to be a long trip.

ONCE AGAIN ALY attempted to focus on the article on her tablet. Normally it was a subject that would have held her interest with ease. The initial reason she'd gone into medicine was a realization that what had happened to her mother hadn't been an isolated case. It was inconceivable to Aly that the United States had the highest maternal mortality rate among developed countries. Her passion had become to understand why over half of the deaths occurred postpartum and what could be done to prevent them.

Over time she'd built a reputation for partnering with companies to develop female-specific diagnostic technology. To stay ahead of the curve, she read medical studies voraciously. She'd never be wealthy, because she used the income she made from her designs to further fund research around the world.

She was not the type of woman to fawn over movie stars or put much value in the superficial. Dylan Sutton was everything she had no interest in—all wrapped up in one incredibly tall, impressively muscled, above average delicious body. He had the classic strong jaw, eyes a woman could lose herself in, and dark blond hair. Although he was nearly two years older than Connor, they shared enough physical characteristics that most thought they were twins. Add a little fame and women literally threw themselves at both men, even though Connor was soon to be married.

Fools.

Men who can have any woman don't settle for one.

Aly glanced at Connor who was chuckling over something Angelina said to him. Okay, there were exceptions to the rule. If Connor were a dog, he'd be a Labrador—always happy, always friendly, loyal to the core. It was impossible to not like him.

Her attention shifted to Dylan again. She blamed her wandering eye on a flaw in the jet's lounge design. With the seats lining the sides in a U-shape, it was impossible to not constantly be aware of what the other passengers were doing. Thankfully he hadn't chosen to sit beside her or she would have gotten nothing done.

As she watched Dylan bend his head so he could hear something Claire said, a flush warmed her cheeks and her grip on her tablet tightened. Of all the things Dylan did that she found grating, his ability to turn her on topped the list. And that he did it effortlessly was truly unsettling.

Raised in a quiet household by a father who taught part-time at Weill Cornell Medicine and still worked as an electrophysiologist in New York City, Aly was more comfortable participating in a medical peer review than attending a social event. A woman in her mid-twenties, she was experienced when it came to men and sex, but neither had done much to hold her interest in the past. If she ever did marry, it would be out of a sense of duty. Her father often said that intelligent people needed to procreate as prolifically as those with lower IQs to keep a balance in the population. Her life plan included finding a well-educated, socially conscious, kind man to settle down with.

Before then, if she required sexual release, there were always toys or the occasional hookup with men she met through her work. Intelligent men understood that sex need not be confused with emotion or commitment. It was a biological function of all healthy humans of a certain age. A person's sex drive was determined mostly by their level of testosterone or estrogen as well as a few other less tangible factors.

Like whatever it is that makes Dylan attractive to me.

The man can't say the word vagina without laughing.

As if sensing her attention, Dylan looked across at her. Their gazes met and held. Regardless of all the reasons she believed it shouldn't, her heart began to race. Her breath became shallower and there was a little flutter in her chest. A fucking flutter. She narrowed her eyes out of irritation with herself.

I should just have sex with him and be done with it.

She mentally charted her cycle and blamed it for her enhanced attraction to a visibly strong man. There was a reason why the study of human sexuality was such a complicated field. Although she had little interest in them, recent studies supported the theory that chemosignaling played a role in sexual responses.

Fundamentally, regardless of how much one might want to deny it, people were still mammals—still operating on instinct and behaviors driven by their biological design. Those factors were the only rationale for Aly's body having a mind of its own when Dylan was around.

Funny how arbitrary life could be at times. The only reason Aly was on Clay Landon's jet, flying off to watch Dylan on the set of his latest movie, was because her two best friends were marrying into this mix. Angelina's engagement to Connor had drawn Aly and Joanna into the group. Joanna's relationship with Bradford, a good friend of the Barringtons, had tightened the bond.

Aly's gaze wandered back to Dylan, who was shaking his

head over something his brother had said, likely something outrageous. Connor was loveable, but he did like to shock people. She could only imagine what he'd say if Dylan ever dated a gynecologist. She groaned. The jokes would never end.

Prior to falling for Bradford, Joanna had considered Dylan a romantic prospect. She'd joked that if she married Dylan and hurried children along, she and Angelina could have offspring that looked similar. Despite her own attraction to Dylan, that pairing had made sense to Aly. Ultimately, though, Joanna's interest had turned to Bradford.

I still worry about them.

Bradford loved Joanna, but he had a dark history that Aly hoped would never endanger Joanna. He and Ian said they sometimes worked for the government but were evasive about what they did. There was an edge to both men that Aly was too realistic to find attractive.

Not that she could see herself with a puppy like Connor.

Or a peacock like Clay.

Dylan met her gaze again and she shuddered as a wave of warmth flooded her. *Oh, hell no. Not him either. Rev up as much as you want, body, but he'd never be more than a guilty indulgence.*

After giving herself a mental shake and Dylan another glare, Aly turned to look out the window. She would have tried to read again, but she was too distracted.

Two hours left.

Then I can put some distance between us and enjoy being on vacation with my friends.

Chapter Two

"HAVE YOU TRIED talking to her?" Claire asked.

"Who?" Her question had come out of the blue and took Dylan by surprise.

Claire lowered her voice. "You know."

No, not falling for that. "I don't."

After a pause, Claire leaned closer. "I can't tell if you really don't know or if you don't want to discuss it."

He smiled. "You've taught me well."

Humor shone in her eyes. "I guess I have." Then her expression became more serious. "It's good to see you doing as well as you are. You look happy. Are you?"

"No reason I wouldn't be. I never saw myself as an actor, but the more I do it the more comfortable I'm becoming with it."

She searched his face. "This movie kept you away from everyone for long enough that we all want to make sure you're okay."

He frowned. "That's what this is about? You're worried about me?"

"No. No." She sighed. "We care about you, that's all.

Connor struggled with finding a balance between who he was and his new fame. How are you handling it?"

"I'm not Connor," Dylan said firmly, but kindly. He took a moment to choose how best to express the difference. By job description, Claire was a life coach. She was more than that, though. She'd become a good friend, a trusted source of advice, and more family than anything else. Few people had had as big of an impact on his life as she had. "Sometimes it does feel like there are two versions of me. Although I like both of them, it can be difficult to navigate the waters where they mix. Connor is funny as hell and when we're alone we're who we've always been—and it feels good. When I'm away from him, I'm—"

"More dignified?"

"I was about to say free but that doesn't sound the way I mean it." He rolled his shoulders backward. "All this acting has made me realize that we also play roles in our daily lives. Some we write ourselves, some are written for us."

Claire's eyes rounded. "Deep."

His smile twisted. "And unexpected. I know. I have played the strong clown most of my life. It worked for where I was and what I needed to be. My path before the Barringtons was clear. Connor and I didn't need college. We both intended to take over our father's business and we would have done well there. I didn't ask for my life to change, but when it did I saw it as an opportunity to discover what else I could be."

Claire blinked a few times fast. "That's beautiful."

Feeling a little self-conscious, Dylan shrugged. "I don't

know about all that, but it's why I chose this movie and to do it on my own. I've had time to see who I'd be away from everyone else."

"And?"

"And I like this version of me as well. Don't get me wrong, there are parts of being famous I could do without, but you prepared me for most of what I've encountered."

Claire gave his forearm a quick squeeze. "I like it as well. Just don't turn your back on all the things that made you wonderful before."

"I won't."

She gave him another long look. "Are you concerned about having Connor on the set of this movie?"

She was the only one who might understand why he didn't have a quick answer to that. There was nothing in the world more important to him than his family. Hell, if they needed him to, he'd walk away from his movie deal, weather the legal battle that would follow, and give up his new career to do what needed to be done.

But if Connor had a few drinks and told the movie crew about any of the shit the two of them had done as kids . . .

"I'll speak to him," Claire said.

Dylan opened his mouth to say it wouldn't be necessary, then decided it might be best to let her. She had a soft way of bringing a person around. Dylan nodded once in place of saying anything. He didn't want his brother to feel judged, but Connor had always been impulsive.

When he'd streaked naked across the football field, it had been Dylan who had punched the snot out of anyone who would have given him shit for it. When Connor fucked his way through everyone's sister in their town, Dylan had met the angry brothers at the end of the driveway. Connor had no idea that the blessed life he'd lived had been possible only because he and Viviana had held the wolves at bay.

Connor blissfully walked through life loving everyone, confident that everyone would love him back. Dylan had only held back once, early on, hoping dealing with a bully himself might toughen Connor up, but Viviana had stepped in.

Bar fights? It was nearly impossible to drink with Connor and not get into one. Dylan had never thrown the first punch, though, and in his heart didn't condone violence.

He'd never said it to Connor because he'd promised his mother he'd always look out for him, but since being on his own it was nice to only engage in choreographed fights. Fame came with its own expectations, but he felt like he had more control over how he dealt with them than he did when it came to redefining who he was with his family. He never wanted to lose his bond with Connor, but Dylan was more than the meathead his brother saw him as.

He was more than the stupidest thing he'd ever done, more than every mistake he'd ever made. Life on his terms, accepted for who he was now—that's what he was looking for.

Claire touched his arm again, bringing his attention back to her. "Angelina, Joanna, and Aly are each so different but I can see why they're friends. Joanna is a healer and both Angelina and Aly were each a little broken. Connor was just what Angelina needed."

Dylan glanced at Angelina who was laughing with Connor then Aly who still had her face averted toward the window. "I don't see either of them as broken."

"Perhaps broken is the wrong word. Hurt? Lost? Yearning for someone of their own? Someone they can trust."

A sound of doubt burst out of Dylan. "Aly would be the first to tell you she doesn't need anyone."

Claire raised an eyebrow. "People tell me all sorts of things I don't believe. You once told me you'd rather die than wear a suit."

Dylan laughed. "I did say that."

"Yes, you did. Notice how Aly chose to sit by herself? She doesn't yet feel confident that she's one of us. And her friend hasn't noticed that because she's still in the smitten stage with Connor."

Dylan cocked his head to one side while looking at Aly through fresh eyes. "So she's hiding in her tablet."

"Probably wishing one of us would go over there and talk to her."

"You should do it. She doesn't like me."

"I don't believe that, but even if that were true, I'm confident you could change her mind." She rubbed a hand over her temple. "Plus, I might close my eyes and try to nap before we land."

Dylan put his hand over hers. "I know better than to ask what you're worried about that we aren't supposed to know, but I'm here if you need me. Whatever is going down, you tell Ian and Bradford they aren't alone."

Her smile was strained. "Hopefully it's nothing, but you have no idea how much I love you for saying that. You're a good friend, Dylan; Ian sees that. He teases you, but he knows that I couldn't be safer than I am with this crew." She sniffed. "Now be the hero you play in the movies and go cheer Aly up. She needs someone in her corner."

Dylan groaned. "You couldn't ask me for something simple—like fly the jet blindfolded?"

Claire laughed. "Dylan Sutton, do not let that woman intimidate you. Beneath all those degrees and big talk, she's just a woman and a lonely one at that. I'm not suggesting you ask her out, just be a friend to her. She's going to feel awkward during this trip when both of her friends go off with their men and leave her hanging. Turn on some of that Sutton charm and you'll soon have her smiling."

"If I weren't a better man because of following your advice in the past I would tell you to take a long walk off a short plank."

With another chuckle, Claire gave his shoulder a nudge. "Well then, trust me on this. I've spent enough time with Aly to really like as well as admire her. She's an intelligent woman, but that doesn't mean she's doing any better at this life game than the rest of us. My guess is her snark will fall away as soon as she feels comfortable around you."

Dylan gripped his armrest and gathered his courage. "I'll go sit with her, but if she slugs me, it's on you."

"You'll be fine," Claire said with humor.

"Sure, said by someone who is remaining safely over here."

OUT OF THE corner of her eye Aly saw Dylan rise to his feet again. If the amount of laughing that had come from the other side of the plane was anything to go by, he'd cheered Claire up.

She grudgingly admitted to herself that he wasn't all bad. Their gaze met and he smiled. She didn't smile back. *Go on back to your brother.*

His smile wavered, then returned in full force.

Oh, shit, he's coming over here. She scrambled to pick up her tablet again. The screen had locked and she was still unlocking it when Dylan plopped into the seat beside her.

"Mind if I join you?"

"A little late to ask since you already have." She hadn't meant for her tone to be quite as cutting as it was. Men didn't make her nervous. No one did. She lowered her tablet and attempted to ignore how good he smelled.

Dylan cleared his throat. "You and I got off on the wrong foot. I've said some things I didn't mean. You said some things you didn't mean."

One comment he'd said to her came back with painful clarity. "You told me if I got laid more it might help me be more likeable." Granted, it was whispered in her ear and not parried across a crowd like most of his insults were, but it had still stung. Between gritted teeth, she added, "For your information I have exactly as much sex as I want to."

Dylan loosened his tie a little and swallowed visibly. "Would you believe I was joking?"

"No." He'd said it to hurt her and although she'd tried not to let it—it had. Briefly. "I don't give your opinion of me much consideration, though, because you also mock my affinity for reading."

Running his hands down his thighs, those incredibly toned thighs, he shifted in his seat. "That's kind of a joke as well. An inside one, I guess. Connor started reading romances and said they changed his life so I just figured you might like them as well."

She looked him right in the eye and with a good deal of sarcasm asked, "Because Connor and I are so similar?"

"No, he's a lot nicer."

Aly's mouth dropped open.

Dylan raised a finger as if asking for a time-out. "I didn't mean to say that."

"It's fine." She told herself it was. It had to be. She wouldn't be the reason the trip wasn't good for either of her friends. "Listen you and I don't have to be friends. I'm okay with that. I do appreciate you coming here to smooth things over. We're good."

He didn't leave as she expected him to. He stayed and after a few minutes said, "We could be."

"What?"

"We could be friends. You and I. If we got past this bumpy part, we might enjoy hanging out." The smile he gave her was warm and charming.

She gave him a long look. This was a side of him she hadn't seen and didn't trust. Why, after all of their sparring, did he suddenly want to play nice? One reason slammed in and she voiced it impulsively. "Oh, I understand. Everyone else is paired up on this trip and you don't want to mix your usual herd of women with your family so you've decided to make do with me. No, thank you."

Dylan whistled. "You're not making this easy."

"Not my problem. I'm sure you can survive without female attention for a few days."

She fully expected him to get up and walk away this time, but he didn't. He folded his arms across his chest and just sat there . . . long enough and quietly enough that the silence began to feel awkward. What did he want? Did he need to hear her say it? "I'm not going to have sex with you." *There, I could not be clearer.*

"I didn't ask you to."

A blush warmed her cheeks as she acknowledged the truth of that. She met his gaze again and hated how she couldn't stay neutral around him. Normally she was the cool head in a group, but add a dash of Dylan and she was either sounding off at him or secretly panting for him. Sometimes she did both simultaneously. It was bad. She didn't walk around announcing to men she wouldn't have sex with them.

Like that's normal to do.

Beneath his sustained attention, her body began to heat. He was crass and immature. He and Connor had once kidnapped Ian, duct-taped him and stuffed him in a laundry basket for God's sake. Every single time she saw him he was with a different woman. Why couldn't her body understand how absolutely unappealing he was?

"I'm glad to hear, though, that you're having just enough sex." When she didn't respond, he added, "That's impressive. I've had not enough and too much, but I've never achieved 'just enough.' I should bring that topic up with my *herd*."

I probably deserve that one. She looked away then back. "I shouldn't have said that. Your personal life is none of my business."

He lowered his arms and turned toward her. "I shouldn't tease you about reading. I didn't realize it was a sensitive subject."

"It's not."

"I don't really have anything against romances. Connor slid me a few and I thought they were well written."

"I don't read romances."

"You might want to give them a try."

Aly's back straightened and she glared at him. "Why is that?"

Dylan lifted and lowered his shoulders. "Who doesn't like a story with a happy ending?"

"I don't require unrealistic expectations to be spoon-fed to me in the form of soft porn."

"Because you like your porn hard core?"

She gasped and he chuckled.

"I'm kidding," he said in a rush. "Truce."

She sat back and they fell into another extended silence.

"You don't watch porn," he said like they were discussing her preference in spices.

"It's disgusting and dehumanizes women into sexual objects."

"So I should watch less." The humor in his eyes was

nearly irresistible.

Images of Dylan and her in a naked, tangled mess flooded in. She took a shaky breath and tried to focus on what they were talking about. "It's not for me to judge what you do with your time."

"But you do—judge me. Constantly. You think you know me, but you don't."

"I—I—" She wasn't sure what to say to that. Her father had always been highly critical of every move she made, but he'd done it because he'd wanted her to excel. She wasn't judgmental, at least not usually, but she couldn't deny that she didn't have the greatest impression of Dylan. *I just need to do a better job of keeping my opinion of him to myself.* She didn't believe in intentionally ever making someone feel bad about themselves. "I'm sorry. You're right, we've both said things we regret."

His smile was easy. "See, we can do this." He leaned closer, close enough to get Aly's body humming for him. "We're already making progress."

Aly studied his expression. There was nothing there to suggest his intentions involved anything beyond what he was suggesting. "Toward being friends."

He nodded slowly. "We should at least try. We'll be hanging out a lot on this trip. I don't know about you, but I don't want to spend the whole time tiptoeing around you. We'll both be more comfortable if we're cool with each other. Plus, I've never invited anyone to come watch me on set before but I'm actually glad you all agreed to. It means a lot to me that you're here."

"I—"

He raised a hand. "Don't say you're not here for me because then I'll say something stupid in response and we'll be right back to where we started. Just say thank you."

A small smile did pull at her lips that time. He was right. That's exactly what would have happened. Friends? Maybe moving him over to that category would cool her response to him. "Thank you."

"You're welcome."

They sat side by side in their first comfortable silence. She picked up her tablet and was about to unlock its screen when he asked, "You really don't watch porn?"

She let her cocked eyebrow and steady stare be her answer. She was not about to go there with him. It was already too easy to imagine having sex with him.

He grinned. "I just thought that with you being an expert on female anatomy you might."

She gave him another long look.

He rubbed the back of his neck as if in thought. "But I guess someone who looks at them all day for work wouldn't want to watch them in action for fun."

She just continued to hold his gaze.

As if realizing he might have wandered down a road he shouldn't have, he stood and said, "I'm going to head back over to my seat so I'll have my stuff next to me when we land."

She should have let him go at that. They were good. No more tension, but they still had clear boundaries. It was just as it should be. When he took a step away, however, she said,

"Dylan."

He stopped and turned back toward her.

"Thank you for coming over to talk to me. You're right, it will make the trip easier if we're getting along."

"Friends?" He held out his hand for her to shake.

Her body went all kinds of crazy haywire when his hand closed around hers. Of all the men she'd known, none had ever made her crave them. Her hand shook slightly in his as she realized that's what he was—a dangerous craving.

The only thing worse than wanting a man from her small social circle despite how wrong he was for her, would be to complicate that situation by having sex with him. She was carefully methodical by nature and being intimate with Dylan would be choosing chaos. With some men she might be able to move on and pretend nothing happened, but something told her that would not be the case with Dylan.

"Friends," she said with a forced smile.

It was the only course of action that made any sense.

Chapter Three

H AD DYLAN PLANNED the details of their trip they would have flown over on a regular airline with first class seats only because he did need to be more careful now that he was in the public eye. Clay's wife, Lexi, had offered to set everything up, and frankly it had been a relief. Prior to the Barringtons, Dylan's experience with vacations had involved a tent and a roll of toilet paper—and he'd enjoyed them. Things were different, and when Clay was involved, beyond luxurious.

Several steel-gray Land Rovers met them at a private airfield. Luggage was magically whisked away by a team of men in dark suits and sunglasses. Clay and Lexi went in one Rover, Connor and Angelina in another. Dylan chose the front passenger seat in the third vehicle, allowing Claire and Aly to sit together in the back.

Claire was quietly texting on her phone. Aly seemed to be enjoying the scenery. Straight out of the airport, the road was flanked by a fjord on one side that had a small town jutting out into the water with the backdrop of a mountain behind it. The other side was a moss-covered hill. Dylan turned in his seat to address Aly and Claire. "The road is about to get a little bumpy. Summer in the Westfjords is really the only time of year this area is accessible, so it's not as touristy and the roads aren't as well maintained as you might see near the cities. As we drive, imagine that we're tracing the edge of Iceland. We'll head out to each peninsula's end then back in along a fjord and out again along another peninsula."

Claire looked up from her phone. "What's the difference between a bay and a fjord?"

Without taking her eyes from the view, Aly said, "A fjord is technically a bay that has steep sides or a cliff. It's formed via ice segregation when a glacier moves through a valley and carves out the bedrock. It's usually U-shaped and can be deeper than the surrounding ocean. In contrast a bay usually has a large mouth that accesses a larger body of water. It can be formed by glaciers, but many were a result of plate tectonics. For example, when Pangea broke along an indented fault line, some of the largest bays in the world were created."

"Glaciers," Claire said. "They sure do beautiful work."

Aly continued, "Interesting fact: much of Iceland has been underlain by permafrost for over a thousand years which has facilitated the stability of those moss slopes."

Dylan and Claire exchanged a look. He considered tossing out a tidbit he'd learned about the area that might make it seem like he was more knowledgeable about glaciers, but he was enjoying hearing what Aly knew. "I've never heard of ice segregation."

Aly's face became animated. "Me either until I started reading about the area for this trip. It's a geological phenomenon brought about by ice lenses. I find water fascinating because it really is a force of global change. Nothing can withstand it. Take a seemingly impenetrable bedrock. It isn't. All water needs is a small pore or a tiny crack. It fills in those spaces and as long as the conditions remain favorable for it, more and more ice will collect and form a lens. It often causes something called a frost heave, but that's a misnomer because frost occurs from water in the air when water vapor—" She stopped. "Sorry, I love to learn new things but you probably don't care about the technical stuff."

"I wouldn't have asked if I didn't want to know," Dylan said. "I understand how you feel, though. I spent most of my life working on large machinery and I can diagnose the cause of intermittent versus function failure. I can list failure patterns and design preventative maintenance plans for them, but a lot of people don't care to know how things work. They just want the end result. I, on the other hand, like to understand the process. I spent some time with a geologist when I first got here and learned a lot about deglaciation. She was equally excited about land formations."

"But she didn't mention ice segmentation?" Aly asked.

"We didn't do a whole lot of talking." He made a face. "I'd introduce you, but things got a little complicated between us."

"Let me guess—*after* you had sex," Aly said.

Dylan's face warmed. "Something like that."

Claire covered her eyes with one hand then rubbed her

forehead.

Dylan's mood took a bit of a dive when Aly shook her head and returned her attention to the passing view.

Her judgement of him hung heavy in the air and he was done with it. "I guess she didn't want to be a member of my *herd*."

Aly's head snapped around and she glared at him. "Do you blame her for that? No woman wants to be one of many."

He waved a hand in the air. "I'm single. *She* asked *me* out. I said yes. We didn't make promises to each other. We were both perfectly free to have sex with anyone we wanted to." He frowned. "I had no way of knowing the next woman I was with was her sister. One of them should have said something."

"Oh. My. God."

I probably shouldn't have shared that last part. Aly was a member of his circle of friends, though, and he wanted to relax when he was out of the public eye. "They looked nothing alike. I never saw them together. Trust me, now I ask for last names."

Aly looked away. "None of this surprises me."

Dylan made a sound of frustration deep in his throat. He didn't know why her opinion of him mattered, but it did. "Hey, before you get all judgey again, I don't see a guy next to you. Maybe you're doing better than I am, but I highly doubt it."

"I am definitely doing better than you are."

"Really? Who was he? This last wonderful man you

fucked?"

Claire intervened, "Dylan, I don't really think this is—"

Aly leaned forward. "He was a neurosurgeon."

"Wait, wild guess, he was married."

A near growl came from Aly as she sat back. "I asked about his marital status, but he lied to me." She hugged her arms around her and snapped, "I wasn't alone, he fooled half the nurses on the floor."

Despite the heat of the moment, a sadness in Aly's expression stopped Dylan from voicing his initial comeback. She'd been hurt by the experience and that realization brought out a protective side of Dylan. "It happens."

She blinked a few times then seemed to relax. "Like accidentally sleeping with sisters?"

He turned his most charming smile on her. "Just like that."

With a hint of a smile pulling at her lips, she asked, "You've been here for months, are there any women you haven't been with?"

"One or two." This time he winked. "But I'm working on that."

She rolled her eyes skyward, but there was growing amusement in them. "Don't drag your feet. Filming wraps up after this trip, correct?"

"It does." He almost turned back around to face forward, but felt he needed to say, "Hey, Aly. It might take us a bit to figure each other out, but it'll get easier. I like to joke, and I may overshare at times, but I'm harmless. I'm looking for nothing beyond friendship with you. In fact, trying to picture the two of us together makes me chuckle. Can you imagine—?"

Claire slapped his arm. "Dylan, is that the lodge we're staying at?"

Dylan turned to see what she was referring to. "No, ours is much larger."

She pointed toward the water. "Which fjord is this?"

Claire kept asking question after question about the area. He had no idea she was so interested, but thankfully he'd been there long enough to have the answers.

Aly remained quiet. In his limited experience with her, that wasn't surprising. She was likely calculating the exact perimeter of Iceland's land mass or something equally cerebral.

He glanced back at her. She was beautiful in a natural sort of way. Her long brown hair was pulled back in a neat, but loose bun. Her face was flawless without the need for makeup. She probably had a lot of doctors chasing after her.

He turned away, frowned, and told himself who she'd been with or would be with in the future had nothing to do with him. What surprised him was how much he disliked the idea of her with someone else.

He glanced back at her again. He wanted to say something to cheer her up, but she was about as easy to get along with as a prickly bush. Behind her, he spotted something, "Hey, look, a puffin."

The car slowed so they could all get a better look. Aly said, "I've never seen one in person." She smiled at him and his heart did a funny little flip. "Thank you."

That was all it took for his cock to decide she might have potential. He turned forward quickly and told himself not to be an idiot. They were on their way to being friends and even that was a Herculean task.

Fucking her?

That would be a mistake.

ALY WAS STILL mentally lecturing herself as their caravan of Land Rovers pulled up the driveway of a sprawling lodge. Perched on the side of a hill, it was the sole building in sight, a wooden structure, slightly weathered, but with an extensive deck that surrounded a mostly glass front. The view on all sides was breathtaking and rustic, but with staff who poured out of the building as soon as the vehicles parked.

Dylan was out of the car as fast as the driver was, opening the door for her. She thanked him and swore to herself she'd do better around him. *I am too intelligent to reduce myself to bickering with him every time we engage. He calls me judgey.* Aly cringed as she replayed some of what she'd said to him in her head. *I am around him. I don't want to be. God, I'm becoming everything I don't like about my father.*

Aly loved her father. He was a brilliant doctor, but there had been times in her life when it had been difficult to like him. Regardless of what she'd achieved, he had yet to tell her he was proud of her. Funny how, no matter how old she got, she never stopped hoping he would.

And Dylan? I really need to get my head straight about what we are to each other. He just made his feelings about me clear. I need to chill out.

At her side as if they were already the friends he claimed he wanted them to be, Dylan said, "I haven't stayed here, but I've heard good things about the place. No better way to see the northern lights, although this is technically not the best time of year to try to. We'll have daylight till almost midnight, then sunrise around three a.m. So if you want to sleep late, make sure you've closed your curtains."

"The place looks amazing and thanks for the tip," Aly said.

Clay and Lexi waved for them to join them. Connor bounded up with Angelina in tow. "Check out that enormous hot tub. We are definitely hanging out in that later. Change my name to Raisin Sutton because I'll be one by tonight."

Smiling, Angelina said, "That's quite a visual, hon."

He looped an arm around her. "I can't wait to make you Mrs. Raisin Sutton."

They kissed and murmured something to each other. Aly was happy for her friend, but standing there and watching them wasn't easy. She put a few feet between them under the pretense of checking out the view.

Dylan followed her. "I have tomorrow free. Is there anything you're excited to see while you're here? I can arrange any tour you'd like."

She looked from him to the rest of the group and back. It no longer felt like he was coming on to her. So, what was this? She searched his face. "You don't have to entertain me, Dylan. I'm happy just being here. I've always been pretty independent."

He pocketed his hands in his jacket and rocked back on his heels. "Independent is good, but it's also nice to share new experiences with someone. I made a list of things the locals suggest people see while here. There's a waterfall not too far away that's over three hundred feet high. They say it's worth the trip. There's a beach with orange and maybe pink sand. I don't know, but that's what I hear. It's supposed to be beautiful. And there are hot springs—natural ones, some that only the locals know about. Hiking, kayaking, whale watching, four-wheeling. I took a helicopter tour when I first got here and it was really cool."

He was trying so hard she felt bad about every less-than-kind thing she'd ever said to him. While looking out over the water, she inhaled deeply then said, "I'm sorry about the stuff I said in the car. I don't know what gets into me sometimes."

He took a moment before answering. "Change isn't easy—for any of us. I imagine you were comfortable with your friends in one setting, then you were whisked into a whole new world with them. Everything's different whether or not you want it to be."

She glanced at him, then away. It was unsettling how accurately he was describing her feelings. Hopefully he didn't read all of her thoughts that easily. Angelina called out that the group was going inside. Aly waved for them to go without her. "I've never seen Angelina so happy."

"The same is true for Connor."

"That kind of connection is rare."

He shrugged. "I guess."

"Have you ever been in love?" She groaned and kicked herself for not holding that question in.

He shook his head. "Never. But I know it's possible. My parents had that."

The wind blew, sending a chill through Aly. Most of what she knew about Dylan she'd learned via Angelina when she talked about Connor. "You lost your mother when you were young."

"Yes."

She hugged her arms around herself and looked back out over the water. "We finally have something in common. My mother passed away from a postpartum complication. It shouldn't have happened. It was completely preventable."

"My mother was ill for a very long time, but I remember her before she was sick and those are the memories I hold on to."

He said it simply but with such sincerity that Aly found herself blinking back tears. "I have no memories of my mother."

"But you still miss her."

His words gutted her. She'd never let herself truly admit the yearning she still had for even one memory. "I do."

He sighed. "Me too." After a pause, he said, "So you became a doctor because of your mother."

She nodded. It might have been fatigue from the trip that had her feeling emotional, but in that moment she and Dylan shared a connection unlike one she'd formed with a man before. Joanna and Angelina were good friends who knew the best and the worst of Aly, but men were never allowed that close. She'd attempted to let them in before, but they either couldn't or didn't want to take the time to understand the passions that drove her. "I'd like to think it's what she would have wanted me to do."

"I bet it is." He glanced back at the lodge then met her gaze. "My mother asked me to always watch out for Connor and Viviana. I've done my best to do that." He waved a hand in a vague reference to everything. "None of this matters as much as my family."

Her heart began to thud wildly in her chest. He looked as comfortable in his life as a successful Hollywood star as he had noodling the day Connor had asked Angelina to marry him. He could be arrogant and brash, but there were moments like this when he seemed so humble and down to earth. Which side of him was the real one? Why were both so damn appealing?

She circled back to the topic of their conversation. "I love my father, but we get along best when we see each other in small doses. He can be—critical."

Dylan cleared his throat. "That can't be easy."

Her eyes darted back to his and her chin rose. "He holds himself to the same high standard."

Raising both his hands in surrender, Dylan said, "I'm sure he does." When the silence that followed was strained, he added, "If you're okay with being out here alone, I'm going to head in. If I know Connor, he's telling Clay I won't mind sleeping in the basement."

He didn't step away.

They stood there just looking into each other's eyes. Her

traitorous body swayed slightly toward him. He bent until his lips were temptingly close.

She couldn't tell him where her thoughts were heading nor did she want to fight with him anymore. There had to be a way to get beyond this. "You're right, Dylan, I was comfortable with things the way they were and I'm doing my best to be okay with all the changes. Thank you for including me."

His smile started in his eyes. "Sometimes you're pretty damn likeable."

For comedic relief, she narrowed her eyes. "Only sometimes?"

He laughed. "I'm taking the Fifth on that one. Come on, let's get inside. It's cold out here."

She nodded and followed him, but she would have argued about the temperature out there. She could easily have shed a few layers.

Chapter Four

A FTER BEING INFORMED that his bedroom was in a separate area of the lodge, down a hall with only Aly's room as well as an adjoining bathroom, Dylan went in search of Clay. He found him in the main area of the house seated beside the fireplace. He sat across from him.

"Clay, I need to change my room."

Clay looked around. "I'm sorry, do I look like a porter? Change your room."

"I was told the top suite was reserved for Bradford and Joanna."

Clay smiled. "It is. I've had rose petals spread out. Candles placed and ready to be lit. If he doesn't propose to her during this trip, I will hang up my Fairy Godfather wand."

Clay was taking the joke about him being a matchmaker a little too seriously, but Dylan didn't have the heart to tease him about it. For someone rich enough to buy and sell the Barringtons, Clay still tried harder than he needed to be accepted. Dylan was grateful to Clay for all he'd done for him, but the friendship they'd formed had nothing to do with his money. Some might say Dylan liked Clay despite it.

Clay was a good guy, but he wielded his wealth like a superpower and there were times when that was a bit much.

"I'm serious, Clay. Switch with me."

"Lexi is napping."

"I don't want to bother Claire." Dylan rolled his eyes. "And I'm not knocking on Connor and Angelina's door."

Clay chuckled. "Wise choice. Sounds like your only option is to switch with Aly."

"That won't solve the issue."

Perking up at that, Clay leaned forward. "What issue are we referring to?"

Dylan sighed. "I just think Aly would be more comfortable sharing a bathroom with anyone but me."

A grin spread across Clay's face. "Are you in need of the services of Clay Landon, Fairy Godfather extraordinaire?"

"First, it's a bad sign that you've started to refer to yourself in third person. And no, it's not like that." The last thing Aly needed was Clay making things more awkward for her. Although there had definitely been a moment outside when the temptation to kiss her had been strong, he needed to say something fast to discourage Clay because once that train left the station there was no stopping it. "I have no interest in Aly. Zero. She could not be less my type."

Clay's eyes widened and he waved a hand in the air, but Dylan kept going because, after speaking to Aly outside about how she was still trying to find her footing in the group, he wanted her to be able to relax and enjoy the trip. "Wanting to move my room has nothing to do with her. She and I could be stranded on an island for years alone and nothing would happen. There's nothing between us and I can't imagine there ever could be."

The face Clay made looked pained. "I suppose that's a good thing because she walked up behind you."

Dylan whipped around in time to catch Aly's retreat from the room. "Fuck. Clay, you could have said something."

He twirled his fingers through the air. "You were on a roll."

Slamming his hand down on the arm of his chair, Dylan swore again. The last thing he'd wanted was to hurt her or make her feel uncomfortable. He'd likely done both. Fuck. Fuck. Fuck.

The smirk on Clay's face had Dylan's hands fisting. "You're an asshole," Dylan said.

"Me?" Clay brought a hand to his chest. "I merely asked a question. You could have declined my offer with much less—enthusiasm."

Deep breath. "You're right. This is on me. Shit."

"Look on the bright side, at least now she knows how you feel."

"Yeah." Dylan glanced back at the hallway Aly had disappeared down. He definitely owed her an apology. So much for smoothing things over with her.

He had just risen to his feet with the intention of going to speak to her when Ian appeared from another part of the lodge. "There you are. Clay, is there a reason you're not answering your phone?" Ian demanded as he approached.

Clay took out his phone and frowned at it. "It didn't

ring. Weird." After repocketing it, he asked, "Is there something I should know? You look tense. More tense than normal."

Ian ran a hand through his hair. He looked tired and more than a little frustrated. "It's probably nothing, but on the chance that it's something I made sure we're prepared."

"What's going on?" Dylan asked.

Ian shook his head. "Have either of you heard from Joanna or Bradford? I've been trying to contact them but they're not picking up either."

"Bad service area?" Clay asked with a shrug.

"I have service," Dylan added.

Ian advanced on Clay. "Have you done anything, Clay, that I need to know about?"

"You'll have to be a little more specific," Clay answered in a wry tone. One thing Dylan admired about Clay was that he wasn't intimidated by anyone.

Ian wasn't amused. "In regard to Bradford and Joanna. They should be here by now. Why aren't they?"

Clay's whole demeanor changed. He stood as well. "All of my plans for them revolved around them staying with us. They said they'd be here. Where else would they go?"

Ian began to pace. "I have a bad feeling about this."

"About what?" Dylan had never seen Ian like this. He'd seen him angry, amused, bored, but never worried. "What can we do to help?"

After running his hand through his hair again, Ian stopped and said, "Hopefully nothing will be necessary and this is just a mix-up. Do you remember Daphne? She hired

Claire and was with us at that event? She almost came with us on this trip."

"I remember. She was kind of shy." Dylan's memory of her was vague. He and Aly had been verbally sparring that night as well.

Ian shook his head. "That's not her name, it's an alias. Everything she told Claire was a lie. The deeper I dug, the more connections I found between her and Bradford. I could be wrong, but I believe she's stalking him."

Clay rubbed his chin. "Romantically?"

"No." Ian's tone was curt.

"You think he and Joanna are in danger?" Dylan asked. Bradford was a badass, but anyone could be taken down if snuck up on. Ian knew that all too well.

Ian flexed and fisted his hand. "I don't know, but I'll feel a lot better when I know where the hell they are."

"This is why I track people with my phone," Clay said blandly. When both Dylan and Ian gave him a surprised look, he said, "A Fairy Godfather is only as good as his intel." He took out his phone and opened an app. "Looks like Bradford is still in the air, heading toward England. Hang on, Joanna is on my friend's island. That doesn't seem right."

Ian sent off a text. "No, it doesn't. Bradford would never leave her on her own."

"Not willingly," Dylan added. "Why do I have the feeling you're texting some covert team you flew over with you?"

The look Ian gave him told him that was exactly what he was doing. *Holy shit.* Ian lowered his voice. "Clay, fuel up your jet. Dylan, keep everyone here calm. I don't know what's going on, but I trust the two of you to get Claire and everyone else the hell out of here and to somewhere safe if something goes down."

"Understood," Dylan said.

Clay looked a little shell-shocked. "You don't think I put them in danger, do you? Is this my fault?"

It was a valid question. Ian had reamed Clay recently for sharing one of Bradford's addresses with Dylan and Connor. He'd pretty much told him he was endangering Bradford by exposing him.

"I don't know, Clay. I sure as hell hope not." He began texting again.

Just then Angelina rushed in and over to Ian. She looked flushed and frightened. She waved her phone at Ian. "You need to read this. It's Joanna. She and Bradford are in trouble."

Ian read the message aloud: **This is Joanna. I'm with Bradford on Clay's friend's island. We're in trouble. Caretaker has been murdered. Someone has Bradford. I'm hiding but I'll keep the phone with me. I don't know how many people are here with us. Contact Ian. Get help. This is not a joke. Please help us. Hurry.**

Ian instantly began to type back. Claire joined the group, standing quietly beside Ian. She was as pale as Angelina was, but they both looked a lot calmer than Dylan felt. Connor appeared and put his arm around Angelina.

No one spoke.

No one breathed.

Ian switched to texting on his phone, then pocketed

them both and turned to Claire. "Everything is going to be okay. No one is better prepared for something like this than Bradford and me. I have a bird in the air with some of the best trained men I know on their way to the island. I have to go." He kissed her.

She clung to him for a moment. "Bring them back safe, Ian." Then she released him with a sniff.

"I will," he swore. The sound of a helicopter landing just outside the lodge was his cue to leave and he bolted out to meet it.

The silence that followed his exit was long and heavy.

A movement across the room caught Dylan's attention. Aly was walking toward them tentatively. "Did something happen?"

Angelina rushed toward her, wiping tears from her cheeks as she went.

THERE ARE MOMENTS in life that freeze time and dwarf everything else. Aly met Angelina in the middle of the room, and comforted her with a hug while she scanned the expressions of the others. Something had happened and it wasn't good. Connor looked as if he might throw up. Clay had a similar expression, although when Lexi joined him he masked his fear and took her aside to talk to her.

As Angelina tearfully updated her, Aly met Dylan's gaze across the room. He was a tougher read, but his face was tight and his eyes tormented. The severity of the situation hit Aly in waves.

"But Ian's on his way to them?" Even to her own ears

Aly's voice sounded calmer than she felt.

Dylan answered, "Just left in a helicopter. He should be there fast."

"A lot can happen in fifteen minutes," Angelina said as she stepped back.

Shaking his head, Clay said, "This is my fault. I brought everyone here."

"There's no way you could have known, hon," Lexi said as she wrapped her arms around him.

"Ian warned me to back off, but I didn't. I wanted what I wanted." His voice was strained.

Dylan stepped toward Clay. "You heard what Ian said about Daphne—or whatever her name actually is—she's been following Bradford for a while. If this is her, she would have done something to him regardless of where Bradford was. I'm guessing this has more to do with him having Joanna with him than anything you did. Before her, he didn't have anything he was afraid of losing."

Both Aly and Angelina gasped in unison. It was an ugly thought, but spot-on. Angelina rushed back to Connor's side. "Oh, my God, do you think this is about hurting Joanna?"

Connor hugged her and shot Dylan a warning look. "Don't think like that. We don't even know for sure it's Daphne who has Bradford."

Dylan looked toward the door then at Clay. "Clay, you heard Ian, get your jet fueled up."

Aly crossed the room to where Dylan was standing and said firmly, "We're not going anywhere without Joanna and

Bradford."

"No one said we are." The easygoing man from earlier was gone. Dylan said, "We don't know what this is. Ian left instructions, but no weapons. He and his men can handle whatever is going down on the island. I have some local connections, but considering we don't know what we're dealing with, I'm not calling anyone yet. We wait, and if Ian says we need to get our asses in the air, that's what we'll do. If he doesn't call, we go to the island, but we don't go alone, and we don't go unarmed."

There was a strength to Dylan that Aly hadn't expected. His confidence brought a calm to the group, even to her. "Okay," she said.

Connor let out an audible breath. "And that's why you're the action hero. I'd follow you into battle."

"Let's hope it doesn't come to that," Dylan said then motioned to Clay who was on his phone texting. "What resources can you bring?"

Clay stood taller. "I don't usually do this kind of thing, but I know people who could organize a small army in hours."

"We might only have minutes," Dylan responded. "But we need a backup plan, and we need one fast."

"On it," Clay said as he typed off a message. "We should get security on the ground here as well."

Dylan nodded. "Definitely, but keep it low-key. We can't do anything that shows Ian's hand before he has a chance to act. For now, everyone have your cell phones with you and gather your passports in case we need to leave."

Connor said, "We should separate into lookout positions until the security gets here. For all we know this was a setup to lure Ian away. They might want Clay."

Clay's eyes widened. "Me?"

Connor shrugged. "You're the one with more money than God. We won't let anyone take you, I'm just saying I don't think anyone is coming for the rest of us."

Lexi's voice went up an octave when she said, "He's right, Clay. You always think nothing could happen to you, but you need to be careful. Maybe now you'll listen when I say we need a bodyguard."

Claire said gently, "There'll be time enough to talk about that later. For now let's do everything we can—and pray."

Dylan walked over and hugged her. "He'll be back, Claire. Ian is the smartest son of a bitch I know. Hell, he brought his own army with him on vacation. Who does that? Not someone I'd want to fuck with. Whoever has Bradford will soon regret that decision."

She shuddered visibly as tears ran down her face. "I'm scared, Dylan."

He hugged her to his wide chest and met Aly's gaze again. "We all are, but we're not alone. And together we're a formidable team." He released her and joked, "Formidable. You taught me not only that word but how to live up to the definition of it. We've got this, Claire."

She wiped the tears from her cheeks as she stepped back. "Okay. Let's gather up our stuff and then choose lookout points."

The smile Dylan gave Claire did funny things to Aly's

heart. She'd watched Dylan save the world in *Danger Doubled*, but here there was no script. No one to impress. This was him. This was real.

Just like her growing feelings for him.

Feelings that had nowhere to go now that she'd heard him clearly state how he felt about her. There'd been no ambivalence in him. He was not interested—a fact that was hard to remember when he came to her side and touched her arm.

"You okay?" he asked.

She nodded and told her body its preference for him was now irrelevant. There were much more important things she needed to focus on.

They began to walk together toward their bedrooms. He glanced down at her. "You're handling this better than the rest of us."

She released a breath she'd been holding in. "Not true, you stepped up and calmed everyone down. That's not an easy feat in a situation like this." She paused and met his gaze. "I didn't mean to imply you'd leave Joanna and Bradford behind."

He put a hand on her shoulder briefly. "You're scared. Me too, but I trust Ian. If there's one thing I know about the Barringtons it's that they protect their own. Ian won't come back without Joanna and Bradford."

"You don't know that. Life isn't a fairy tale where everything has a happy ending." Aly started walking down the hall again. Dylan fell into step beside her.

He put a hand on her arm and pulled her to a stop. "I

know that, and that's why I'm prepared to do whatever needs to be done. I've never enjoyed hunting, but I'm a fair shot. Connor is too. If things get ugly, get in that jet and get out of here."

She pulled her arm away from his touch. "What makes you think I can't shoot?"

"I don't know—the doctor part?"

She frowned and admitted, "You're right. I've never held a gun, but if you think I could fly off to safety while you head to the island, you don't know me."

He gave her a long, steady look. "I'm only a hero in the movies. I don't know how to do this best or even what the hell is going on. Clay and I promised Ian if anything happened we'd get Claire and the rest of you somewhere safe. I won't force you to leave your friend if it comes to that, but I'll make sure you have a way out if you want one."

"You're not a meathead," Aly said, then covered her mouth with her hand. She didn't normally blurt things out, but her emotions were all over the place.

His smile was strained. At the door of her room, he said, "I don't mind the label and sometimes I live up to it. Right now, I don't have that luxury. We need to get our shit and get back out there to meet everyone."

Objectivity was what she'd lost with Dylan. She'd been trying to convince herself there was nothing likeable about him, but if she removed her feelings toward him from the equation—he was just a good man doing the best he could in a tough situation. Her pride was still stinging from earlier, but when compared to Joanna and Bradford being in danger, her feelings were insignificant. "I'll be quick."

"Don't worry about clothes or anything replaceable. Passport. Credit cards. Things you can carry on your person."

"Got it." They separated into their adjoining bedrooms. Aly raced to gather her ID, credit cards, and passport as well as her loose cash from her bags and stuffed them into the pockets of her jeans because a purse could be accidentally left behind.

Dylan met her in the hall when she emerged. "Got everything?"

"I do." Although she'd never been in this particular situation before, she'd learned to keep her head cool in emotional situations—at least where patients were concerned. She strove to summon that clarity for Joanna and Bradford.

They met up with everyone back in the main area of the lodge. Claire entered the room with a female member of the staff. "Everyone, this is Helka. Her boyfriend is a hunter. She called him. He and a few of his friends are on their way here. One has a rifle. They said they'd sweep the area and tell us if anything looks suspicious. I promised I'd gift the group a new fishing boat."

Clay interjected, "Hell, I'll buy them each one. Helka, if nothing that happens here today hits the news, I'll throw in a helicopter."

"He means it," Connor said.

Eyes round, Helka said, "No boats are necessary. No helicopter, either. We'll keep you safe because it's the right thing to do. We pride ourselves on the lack of violence here and no one wants to see that change."

Clay exchanged a look with his wife and Aly almost smiled because she knew what it meant. Helka's humble response had just gained her and her friends a very generous ally.

"There is one thing I would like," Helka said. "Later, when everything settles down."

"Name it and we'll make it happen," Clay answered.

Helka's cheeks reddened. "My friend Freyja is a huge fan of Dylan. She has watched *Danger Doubled* about ten times. If she could meet him even for a moment—"

"Absolutely," Dylan said. "She could come to the set as well if she'd like."

Of course she could. Wouldn't want to leave one local unfucked.

Aly gave herself a mental smack. *I need to get myself under control.*

Helka smiled. "Thank you. She will be so happy." Her phone beeped with a message. "Einar says they are here and see nothing suspicious. There is not much out there to hide behind, so do not worry. They will remain until your friends return."

Aly didn't realize she was shaking until Dylan put his arm around her in support and said, "It's going to be okay. See, we are amateurs and we already have this side handled. Imagine what Ian is capable of."

She nodded, allowing herself the comfort of his support. From the moment Aly had met Bradford she'd known danger would follow him. She'd prayed it wouldn't be him who brought it, but of all the things she'd feared, she hadn't prepared herself for this. "We need to do something."

Dylan gave her back a supportive rub. "Not yet. First we need to give Ian a chance to do what he does."

"What *does* he do?" Aly asked.

No one answered. Outside of Claire, it was likely that no one knew. Aly had asked out of frustration. She'd never been good at sitting back and doing nothing. "I feel so—so helpless."

Angelina came over and took one of Aly's hands in hers. "We all do."

The group huddled closer and she returned to Connor's side. Helka gave them periodic reports on the location and progress of her boyfriend and his friends. It was a solemn, tense stretch of time. All they could do was wait and pray.

When Claire's phone beeped with a message, she picked it up so quickly she nearly dropped it. "It's Ian." She read aloud. "Everyone is safe. Will meet with Interpol before we return but the situation has been resolved."

Aly sagged against Dylan. "They're safe."

He held her to his side. "I never doubted it." Although he spoke with confidence, the shaky breath he released implied otherwise.

Claire continued, "Ian says the man he left here is concerned with the armed locals swarming the lodge." She started texting furiously. When she finished, she held the phone to her chest. "I should have known he wouldn't leave us unprotected. He says his man is in sniper position on the roof. Helka, tell your friends if they spot him, he's on our side."

Helka immediately started typing on her own phone.

"Joanna's pretty shook up," Claire said. "Daphne killed the caretaker of the island, drugged Bradford, and planned to kill Joanna first then Bradford."

"Oh, my God," Angelina said.

Connor hugged her close and kissed her forehead. "They're safe now."

Claire continued, "By the time Ian got there, Joanna had already saved Bradford."

Not surprising. For as long as Aly had known Joanna she'd faced down all threats for those in need of protection. Bradford had better be good to her. "That's our Joanna."

Lowering her phone, Claire added, "Daphne's dead. She tried to take the gun from one of Ian's men and was taken out. That's why they need to meet with Interpol before returning. He's confident it'll be a brief exchange, though."

Relief flooded through Aly as it sank in that Joanna was truly safe. The more the shock of the situation subsided, the more she became aware of every place her body was touching Dylan's. His arm was still around her. Her side was pressed to his. What had been a comfort a few minutes earlier quickly became a sweet torment as her body began to warm.

She reminded herself that regardless of how good it felt to be in his arms, he'd been painfully clear about how he felt toward her. She needed to not only respect that but also stop letting her attraction to him affect how she treated him.

Which will be easier if I put a little distance between us.

Aly slid out from under Dylan's arm and stepped away.

He gave her an odd look she might have confused for him feeling something for her if what he'd said earlier about her to Clay wasn't still ringing in her head. "I don't know about anyone else, but I could use a drink."

"I'd love a beer. Helka, what are we stocked with?" Dylan asked.

"Everything. Would you like local or imported?" Helka answered.

"Local. I'll trust your taste." Dylan nodded toward Connor. "Just a few, though, beer was illegal for a long time in Iceland because it was linked to loud and unsavory behavior."

"Such a killjoy. Don't worry, Dylan, I'm a family man now. I hardly drink anymore." Connor wiggled his eyebrows at Angelina. "Unless someone wants to try some Brennivín with me."

She smiled up at him. "After today, I'd say we've all earned a buzz."

Claire chimed in, "I'll have a large glass of whatever wine you have, Helka."

"I will as well," Aly said.

Clay and Lexi declined, but that didn't surprise Aly. She couldn't remember a time when she'd seen either of them drink.

Dylan waved toward the door. "Helka, would you like to join us? This couldn't have been an easy day for you either. You're welcome to invite your friends in as well. We owe them big."

With a snap of his fingers, Clay announced, "You're

right, Dylan. Helka, consider yourself and your friends our guests tonight." He took out his phone. "I'll have more staff sent over. Relax. Hang out. Tell us all about you and your dreams."

Lexi wrapped her arms around Clay and laughed. "You are crazy, but I love you, Clay." She smiled at Helka. "Please do join us. Clay would like nothing more than to get to know you and your friends and possibly find a way to help more than you'd like him to."

Helka hesitated, then asked, "Could my friend Freyja join us?"

"Absolutely," Clay and Lexi answered in unison.

Helka looked to Dylan as if for confirmation. He didn't immediately answer, but eventually said, "I'd love to meet her."

Aly forced a smile. *Joanna and Bradford are safe. That's all that matters.*

Chapter Five

RELIEF GAVE WAY to a flurry of action as Helka set a drink in everyone's hand then headed outside to speak to her friends. Dylan downed his beer with an enthusiasm he hadn't shown alcohol in a while. He was still settling after a roller coaster of emotions.

Everyone was safe—that was the most important part.

Aly didn't look happy, but she'd gone on the same crazy ride and hers had started with overhearing his conversation with Clay. He knew he needed to address that last part with her, but the glass of wine she raised to her lips shook and he decided it wasn't the best time for that conversation.

Which was probably a good thing because he was still sorting out what the hell he should say.

Aly, remember when I said I had no interest in you? I didn't mean to imply you're not fuckable. In fact, it's beginning to be too easy to imagine us together.

With a self-deprecating smile, Dylan crossed the room to place his empty beer bottle on the tray Helka left on a stand. All the attention from being in movies was getting to his head. Aly had yet to even hint that she was interested in him and what was the likelihood she'd still be thinking about what he said to Clay after hearing that Joanna and Bradford were in danger? *Zero.*

I'm being an idiot. Later, when things calm down I'll make a joke about it, we'll both laugh, and it'll be forgotten.

Aly looked up from talking to Claire and met his gaze. *Oh, she's pissed.* Dylan reached for another beer, opened it, and took a swig without looking away. In some ways she reminded him of the hamster he'd had as a child. Man, that thing had a nasty bite in the beginning. Viviana had brought it home as a gift for Connor and him. At first it hadn't seemed like the best idea to give two hulking teenage boys whose bodies had grown faster than their brains such a delicate pet, but Viviana was always trying to bring out the softer side of the men in her family.

Not an easy feat after their mother died, but Viviana had pushed them to talk about messy things like emotions. She'd made sure the family not only went on, but did it together.

And the hamster? She'd said it would teach Connor and him empathy and how to be gentle. Looking back, her talk might have been in response to the number of fights he and Connor were engaging in, both with each other and the rest of the world.

It wasn't that they didn't have other pets. They'd had a Newfoundland growing up. Best dog ever. They all still missed her, but she was a huge dog, well over a hundred pounds and there'd been nothing gentle about her.

A hamster? Dylan hadn't wanted it.

He remembered, though, the first time he squatted down

to give it a good look and realized it was terrified. Something in him had shifted then. He started looking at their interactions through its eyes and trying to make them less stressful.

He was no fucking hamster whisperer, and when that hamster died he didn't rush out to replace it, but the experience of owning it stayed with him. Viviana had been right about what it had taken for Hammy to trust him—patience and a gentle hand.

Dylan took a swig of his beer and wondered what Aly would think if he told her she reminded him of a tiny rodent. *I probably shouldn't mention that when I apologize about the other stuff.*

As if she could read his mind, her eyes narrowed and she turned away. He took another swig and smiled. Some men might be put off by her bristling personality, but all those glares were beginning to turn him on. He wanted to know what was behind them.

She'd said she had just enough sex. It was an odd claim and one that implied she'd never had amazing sex. You could never have enough of that.

Now, the sex Dylan had been having since becoming a celebrity, that could get old. It was good, but not great. He was getting tired of waking up next to women who didn't know the real him. The more he saw how happy Connor was with Angelina, the less satisfying casual hookups were. Knowing what was possible made sex for the sake of it— empty.

It didn't help that it was also easy for him now that everyone knew his name. In the old days, having meaningless sex had at least required effort. If Dylan never made another movie, his affiliation with the Barringtons and Clay were enough to keep women knocking at his bedroom door.

Helka returned with her friends and the noise level of the room rose. Almost immediately, she escorted a beautiful blonde woman over to meet Dylan. "This is my friend Freyja."

Dylan nodded in greeting. He'd learned that Icelandics didn't love touching upon first introduction. "Nice to meet you, Freyja. I can't tell you how grateful we are to your friends for looking out for us." Helka excused herself to join the rest of the group.

"Can't?" Freyja's smile was truly adorable and held all the friendliness he'd grown accustomed to from the locals. Icelandic women, perhaps because of their Viking heritage, were strong, smart, and independent.

"Just an expression meaning I don't have the words to properly express it." During his time in Iceland, Dylan had grown used to the locals not always getting idioms or jokes, but their English was impeccable. They often spoke several languages.

She looked away, then back, meeting his eyes boldly. "Thank you for letting me join your party."

"It's not quite a party—more of an after-a-good-scare drink or two, but we're happy to have you."

"Helka said you were all so calm she doubts you were ever in any danger."

"Well, we're American. We're used to crazy."

Freyja laughed at that. "Anna and Margret said you were

funny."

Oh, boy. He'd forgotten how everyone knew everyone. "In my defense, I had no idea they were sisters."

Freyja shrugged. "When they told me the story, neither was complaining."

That was something, anyway. Dylan joked and brought a hand across his forehead as if wiping away nervous sweat. "Whew."

Her lips pursed. "In fact, all the good they had to say about you is what made me really want to meet you."

Dylan took another swig of his beer. She was beautiful and interested. Why wasn't he feeling it? He sought out Aly. She was seated on the couch with three of the young men hovering around her. One said something that made her smile.

Dylan frowned. He didn't like the way the men leaned in when they spoke to her.

"I'm too late, I see," Freyja said, bringing his attention back to her.

"I'm sorry?"

Her smile was genuine and she raised her glass of wine. "Are you a couple?"

"Who?" Dylan's attention returned to Aly for a moment. "No."

"She'll come around."

Dylan shook his head. "We're not like that."

"Don't worry. My mother says if a road is essential, elves will always move out of the way."

Elves and trolls. Before spending time in Iceland, Dylan

would have said believing in either was for children. Belief in them, however, was woven through the Icelandic culture. If asked by an outsider many would deny their existence, but few would dare disturb an area where they were known to reside. Much like the local's relationship with the harsh weather of the country, they knew their hidden people could be generous or bring destruction. "I didn't realize elves were matchmakers."

"They are a great many things, but what I mean is that if something is meant to be it will be."

"I agree."

Freyja looked across at Aly. "What do you like about her?"

Dylan considered her question for a moment. "Everything. She's brilliant and dedicated to making a difference. She's snarky, which can be fun. My future sister-in-law is one of her best friends. She's been loyal and supportive of her through the years. Even when she gets a little snippy, it's because she cares. She's just a good person, I guess. And in this crazy world that's not all that common."

Freyja sighed as if in admiration. "You truly are a rare find, Dylan. Most American men would mention a woman's looks first. Many are intimidated by strong women. Do you perhaps have a little Viking in you?" She looked him over. "You certainly have the physique of one."

The idea that he might tickled at his imagination. He puffed out his chest and said, "I have been told I look like the stone troll Karl."

Freyja's laugh rang out. "Well, I hope you find your Kerling."

"Someone literally stuck with me forever?"

"My father would say that's an apt description of marriage."

Dylan chuckled at that. The locals were friendly and blunt, two things that had made Iceland a place he knew he'd return to many times after the movie completed. "I only have a few more scenes to redo, but if your family or friends would like to visit the set, I'll tell the crew to admit you."

"My parents would love that," Freyja said. "My mother has quite the crush on your brother. She said he has the best bare ass in the business."

"I'll tell him that," Dylan joked. He looked down at Freyja's smiling face and marveled that he wasn't tempted. His attention returned to Aly and as soon as his gaze met hers his heart began to beat wildly in his chest. She was not happy with him, but oddly that was okay. *If she's irritated because I'm talking to Freyja, she's not that into any of the guys standing around her.*

His eyebrows rose as a thought occurred to him.

She might like me.

Imagine that.

He shot her a cocky grin that brought a flush of color to her face just before she turned away. *She's totally into me.*

LOOK AT HIM, so proud of himself just because he has another drooling fan.

Imagine trying to have a relationship with someone who is constantly in need of that kind of attention.

"You know, having sex with me would be the perfect way to make him jealous," the young man beside her said.

The man beside him said, "A dip in the hot tub with me would achieve the same results. Suits optional."

Aly turned her attention back to the men surrounding her. They were great examples of how healthy an active, outdoor lifestyle was. Not just physically fit, but comfortable with themselves and their sexuality.

One of the men said, "Don't embarrass her. I dated an American once. They're not as open as we are about sex or nudity."

"That's not true," Aly denied. "I am completely comfortable with both."

"Really?" the man next to her asked. "Have you been to a pool here yet?"

"I have not." Aly vaguely remembered reading that the norm was to shower naked before entering the waters and that the facilities lacked stalls. She'd also read that Icelandics in general were comfortable enough to swim in the nude even in groups. She considered lying about her comfort level with either then said, "Okay, I'm your stereotypical repressed, shame-filled, never-to-be-seen-naked-in-public American."

The group around her burst out laughing. When they settled, one of the men said, "Helka said you're a doctor."

"I am."

"Do all of your patients remain fully clothed while you treat them?"

"No, but there's a sheet covering all but the necessary

area."

The man closest to her looked fascinated. "So even with a doctor Americans are embarrassed by the natural body?"

"I'm sure not all." Aly shrugged and had to concede, "It's cultural."

He shook his head. "I can't imagine. It's a sexualization of something that need not be. We have public showers without stalls. So many tourists come and want to shower with their bathing suits on. In my opinion it is more important to be clean and healthy than to be hidden and filthy."

He had a point. "I haven't put much thought into it."

The man next to him said, "As a doctor, you should. My family travels often. My sister went to uni in the UK. She said she relaxes when she comes home. The English don't understand her comfort with nudity and openness about her sexuality. Everyone has sex, yes? Everyone has the same parts. What is the purpose of all the shame?"

It might have been a result of the second glass of wine she'd downed quickly, but Aly found herself agreeing. "I have to say in my head I am one hundred percent in agreement, but culture is so internalized I don't know how easy it would be to turn off my public inhibitions."

One of the men said, "Spending time with nature will change your mind. I'll send you directions to some safe geothermal pools remote enough that you might have some privacy. Don't just hop into any pool you come across. Some are full of bacteria, some are deceptively hot beneath the surface. Others are known to heat with no warning. Nature makes few promises of kindness. People have been burned. However, there are a few we trust enough to recommend."

"I'd like that. Thank you." It really was interesting to be with men who could discuss sex, offer sex, and not be overtly sexual. Although offers had been tossed out, Aly didn't feel uncomfortable with them and not one of them was crowding her or giving her a reason to be concerned. Iceland was known for being one of the most gender equal societies and she could see that. The thought of going swimming without a suit had her glancing over at Dylan again. He and Connor towered over every other man in the room. Any woman would have been attracted to either.

Dylan looked a little less pleased with himself than he had earlier. The man beside her said, "You look at him so much even I want you to be with him."

Aly blushed and looked away from Dylan. "We're not like that."

"If he doesn't see how you feel about him, he's as blind as a bookless man."

It was a phrase she'd never heard, but the meaning was clear. "He's an attractive man, that's all. And, trust me, he doesn't feel the same. I'm sorry, I'm sure you don't want to hear this. It's been a long day and I'm emotionally all over the place. My friend is coming back soon and I can't imagine the state she'll be in."

The man on her right nodded to his friends. "Meeting you, Aly, has been a pleasure. I hope your friends are okay." He stood. The others rose to their feet as well. "Should you find yourself in need of a tour guide, send a message through

Helka and I'm sure one of us will be free."

Aly stood as well. That would never happen, but it was flattering that the option was there. She addressed the men in general. "Thank you so much, both for coming to our rescue as well as for the conversation."

"You're welcome," the men echoed, then one called to Helka in Icelandic. She agreed in English. Freyja joined her and the group made their way toward the door. As she passed Aly, Helka stopped and lowered her voice. "I told Clay and Lexi that inviting us in was enough of a gift. We don't require more. I didn't want to offend him, but I wanted to be clear."

Aly looked over at the smiling couple. "I can't guarantee he won't still send you something, but he only wants to help."

Helka nodded. "At first I thought he was a braggart, but after talking to him I think he doesn't know how else to connect to people. I like him."

That pretty much summed up Aly's experience with Clay. "Me too. Thank you again for today."

Freyja's smile was warm. "It's always interesting to meet an actor. Many are not as amazing in person as they are on the screen. Dylan did not disappoint."

I'm sure he didn't.

"That's great. He's a very nice man." None of it was a lie. Okay, maybe just the part about where Aly said it was great that Dylan and Freyja had gotten along so well.

Freyja and Helka exchanged a look, then Helka said, "We hope you enjoy your time here. Claire has my information. Don't hesitate to reach out if there is anything you need."

"We will."

In the quiet after the group left a tension returned. Without the distraction of the visitors the reality of what had brought them together came crashing back in. Angelina came over. "Are you okay?"

Aly smiled. "How could I not be after spending time with that hot group of men?"

Lies don't fool best friends. Angelina touched Aly's arm. "I'm worried about Joanna too."

Aly slumped then sat in the chair behind her. "She's one tough cookie, but I can't imagine how scared she must have been."

Angelina joined her. "The waiting is the part that's killing me, I just want to fly to her and give her the biggest hug. I already called Whitney, just to hear his voice. I know he's fine, but I had to hear it."

Angelina's son was with her parents and could not be safer, but Aly completely understood. "Considering how things played out, aren't you glad you didn't take him on this trip?"

"Absolutely. I was tempted to, but Connor said we'd come back with him after we're married when Dylan isn't working so we can spend more time together. I wonder if Joanna will want to go back to the States tonight? It would be a shame to come all this way and see nothing, but I think we should all go back with her if that's what she wants to do."

"I agree." Aly reached over and took Angelina's hand in hers. She had no idea how she'd lucked out and brought these women into her life, but she was immensely grateful to have them. She could be real with them without fear of them judging her. With that in mind, she leaned closer and said, "I have a small problem."

In a voice just above a whisper, Angelina asked, "What is it?"

"I may have feelings for Dylan."

"Nooooooo." The round-eyed shock was too forced to be believed.

Aly dropped her hand and gave her a light smack in the side. "I'm serious. It's ridiculous. He has no interest in me. I'm a doctor for God's sake. He's the opposite of my taste in men. Why am I acting like a twelve-year-old with my first crush? I get that attraction is complex and can defy logic, but Dylan reduces me to . . ."

"You're human." Angelina made a sympathetic sound. "I have learned to be kinder to myself recently. I wasted so much energy trying to live up to someone else's standards and never feeling like I could. Then came Connor who loves me for who I am. I'm not a different person than I've ever been, I'm just more grounded now. Someone told you you weren't enough, Aly, but they were wrong. Relax. You might think Dylan isn't interested in you—"

"He said it himself."

"Oh." Angelina made a pained face. "Well, either way, you're allowed to feel how you feel." She leaned in. "Besides, I don't believe he meant that for a second."

"It doesn't really matter. I've considered having sex with him just to get him out of my system, but I'm worried I might wake up and like him more."

Angelina chuckled. "The horror."

"I'm serious."

The sound of someone clearing their throat behind the couch made both women jump and turn. Dylan stood there with a carefully blank expression that left Aly wondering if he'd heard the last part of their conversation.

If he had, he wasn't giving any indication of it. *Perhaps because he has zero interest. Zero. You don't get less interested than that.* He said, "Ian called. They're on their way back. ETA five minutes. Joanna is still pretty shaken up so it's a good thing everyone left."

Both Angelina and Aly stood. "How is Bradford?" Aly asked.

Dylan lifted and dropped a shoulder. "Ian said he's taking it hard as well. He feels responsible."

Aly's father would have said he was. Aly might have as well but she was becoming aware how often her father's quick criticisms framed her views. Aly was not only hard on herself, but also to those around her—well, outside of Angelina and Joanna.

Why? Because I love them and love shouldn't be judgmental.

The thought floored Aly. She thought about her past relationships and how easy it had been to fall into a pattern of focusing on their shortcomings. It was unsettling to also realize that she'd chosen men who had been equally critical of her. *What would it be like to be with someone who loved me just the way I am—flaws and all?*

That's what Angelina found in Connor.

What Bradford found in Joanna.

Angelina stepped away, leaving Aly and Dylan alone. They stood looking at each other for a moment. She wondered what it was that stopped him from being attracted to her. Was it as complicated and unexplainable as how she felt toward him?

He rocked back on his heels. "What a day, huh?"

"You could say that again."

"I feel like dough that has been put through one of those pasta makers."

It was an odd image, but somewhat fitting. Aly shook her head. "Not the trip any of us expected."

"Aly, about earlier, when I was talking to Clay and you heard me say—"

The door of the lodge opened. Aly turned toward it and walked away from Dylan as soon as she saw the shell-shocked expression on Joanna's face. Her friend was hurting and that's all that mattered. Angelina must have felt the same way because the three met in the middle of the room and simply hugged.

There was a smudge of mud on Joanna's chin and a cut beside her eyebrow that looked like her skin had split from a punch. "Why don't we go to my room and get you cleaned up?" Aly suggested.

Joanna nodded.

Aly took one glance at Bradford and her heart broke for him. He looked devastated. She hesitated for just a moment then went to him and gave him a hug. He didn't hug her back, but she would have sworn she saw his eyes mist over. Right there, that was the moment she decided he was family too. She took a step back and said, "I'm glad you weren't hurt."

He gave one curt nod.

She smiled up at him gently. "We've got Joanna. Go have a drink."

As she headed back to Joanna and Angelina, Aly caught Dylan watching her. His expression was difficult to decipher, but his eyes burned with something that brought a flush to her cheeks. She told herself she was imagining it, but that didn't stop her heart from fluttering as well.

Friends, that's all he wants to be. Stop reading something into every look.

Distracted, Aly walked right into Joanna.

"Is she okay?" Joanna asked.

As the three of them made their way toward Aly's room, Angelina said, "She may have feelings for Dylan."

"Noooooo," Joanna said, smiling for the first time since she'd walked in. "I had no idea."

Aly rolled her eyes skyward. How was it that even after a near death experience, her friends didn't miss an opportunity to give her shit? "I'd be nicer to someone who is about to clean up your face."

Joanna's hand went to the small cut beside her eyebrow and her eyes darkened. "I would have killed Daphne if Bradford hadn't stopped me. I didn't think I was capable of killing anyone, but I am."

Aly put her arm around Joanna and led her the rest of the way into her room. *What would I want someone to say to me?* "We love you, Joanna. Let it out. We're here for you."

Angelina sat on the bed and encouraged Joanna to take a seat as well. Joanna was too nervous. She stood next to Aly, shaking and reliving the experience on the island. She told them about how she'd found the caretaker dead and seen the drag marks leading away from him. Daphne had shot the caretaker, drugged Bradford, dragged him off to the barn, tied him up, and planned to kill Joanna in front of him. Joanna retold how Daphne's brother had been trafficking and murdering people along the southwest border of the US until Bradford stopped him dead. "She wasn't going to stop," Joanna said. "Had she gotten away with it, she planned to come back and kill our future children. I hate myself for it, but I'm glad she's dead."

Aly hugged her closer. "I'm all about saving lives, but some people are too far gone."

Angelia agreed. "I can't imagine how scared you were."

"I was terrified. Ian told me to hide. I couldn't. I didn't know who had Bradford. I love him so much, more than I ever thought I could love someone. Bradford would give his life for any of us, and I couldn't do less for him."

Blinking back tears, Aly was humbled by the purity of her friend's relationship with her partner. There was no ego, no jealousy—just love. "You found yourself a good man, Joanna."

Joanna met her gaze. "That's not at all what I expected you to say."

Rather than denying the truth, Aly exchanged a look with Angelina then said, "I'm not always right, and I'm learning how to look at situations and people through more than one lens. I thought Bradford was dangerous—"

Joanna took Aly's hand in hers. "You were right to warn me. The things Bradford has survived, the things he has seen and done . . . they're a weight he'll always carry with him. But he's more than his worst moment. He has saved more women and children than he'll ever say, and there's blood on his hands because of it, but I can't see him as anything but a hero. When I had the chance to kill Daphne, he stopped me. He didn't want me to pay the price he has. He's a good man. I'm sorry I hid him away from you both this past month because I was afraid you wouldn't be able to see him the way I do."

Angelina hugged Joanna. "He is so lucky to have found you."

"So are we." Tightening her hand on Joanna's, Aly said, "Bradford is one of us now." She smiled to lighten the mood. "Poor man."

"Thank you." Tears filled Joanna's eyes.

Perhaps to prevent the cry fest that was impending, Angelina said, "Now all we have to do is figure out why Dylan said he's not interested in Aly."

"We don't, actually." Aly waved a hand in the air to dismiss the idea. "I'm emotionally drained."

Angelina winked at Joanna and said to Aly, "Go get your medical supplies. Joanna and I will figure it out."

After looking back and forth between the two of them,

Aly said, "I'm only stepping away because I don't want that cut to get infected or to leave a scar."

Joanna and Angelina moved to sit on the corner of the bed. "We'll be right here."

Aly shook her head as she walked away, but she wasn't irritated with her friends. Honestly, if talking about Dylan brought comfort to Joanna, they could discuss him all night. After picking up the small medical kit she took with her everywhere, Aly paused. Before Joanna had walked in Dylan had been about to explain the very comment Angelina and Joanna were discussing.

At the time it had seemed unimportant in the face of Joanna's distress, but she wondered what he'd been about to say. She cringed as she imagined sitting through an apology where he explained that although he'd meant what he'd said, he hadn't meant for her to hear it. There was a chance he'd been about to admit he hadn't meant it, but she didn't see a reason why he would lie to Clay.

When Aly returned to the bedroom, Angelina announced, "We've got the perfect plan."

Joanna looked exhausted, but she was smiling. "It's brilliant really."

Pulling up a chair so she was sitting in front of her friend, Aly settled her supplies on the bed beside Joanna and took out her antiseptic. "I'm sure it is."

"Did you bring a bathing suit?" Joanna winced when Aly cleaned out her cut, but kept talking without waiting for Aly to answer. "If not, I brought a few."

Angelina jumped in. "There's a hot tub on the deck. After a day like today all you have to do is say you're tense and need to relax. We'll make sure you're alone. If Dylan truly isn't interested he won't join you. But if he's holding back how he feels, he won't be able to resist."

"Sounds like a solid plan, but I can't see myself doing that." Aly applied a small, ointment-covered bandage to the cut. "When you need to change this, come see me. It's not a deep cut, but moist healing is the best way to prevent scarring."

Joanna touched the small bandage and her expression tightened. "As you get to know Bradford and he becomes comfortable around you, you might see his back. It's covered with deep scars he received while trying to save his sister from gang members who were pimping her out. They thought they'd beaten him to death, but he lived to try to save her again. He was never able to. She was still with them when she died of an overdose." She swallowed visibly. "Pretend you don't see the scars. He doesn't want to talk about them."

"Of course," Angelina assured her.

Aly placed her supplies back in her bag. "He's been through so much. Just make sure he never releases that pain onto you."

Joanna nodded. "We've spoken about that. That's my dealbreaker." She lowered her hand. "He said his would be if he couldn't keep me safe." She gripped her hands on her knees. "This wasn't his fault. What if I can't get him to see that?"

Aly opened her mouth to tell Joanna everything would

be okay, but she couldn't bring herself to lie to her. If that was the line Bradford had drawn in the sand, the events on the island might have been enough to convince him that being with Joanna could prove deadly for her. A man like Bradford might walk away rather than risk harm coming to someone he loved.

Angelina was also painfully quiet. Eventually, she said, "Bradford loves you."

"I know that," Joanna said. "I just hope it's enough."

Aly moved to sit in solidarity next to Joanna. It had been a long day for all of them and there was comfort in the simplicity of being together without the need to talk. They sat like that for an extended amount of time, then Joanna slapped her hands on her knees. "I do think the hot tub idea would work. And no one would think it odd for you to want to be out there. I'd soak in it myself if I thought I could keep my eyes open. I feel—deflated."

"That's natural," Aly said. "Your body needs to replenish its energy. You just went through a trauma. Honor the process of working through it."

Angelina stood. "I didn't understand the destructiveness of stress until I started working for Connor. Remember how bad my last job was? I was tired all the time. I feel ten years younger." She smiled. "Rest and great sex—I highly recommend both for their healing powers."

Joanna chuckled. "I'll keep that in mind." She sighed and stood as well. "Thank you for this. I can't say I feel better, but I do feel less out of control."

"That's what friends are for," Aly said.

After pausing for a moment in front of Aly, Joanna said, "Relationships are complicated and scary. They come without promises and more questions sometimes than answers. But they're worth it. Bradford is worth all of this and so much more."

Angelina joined them. "Dylan might not be the one for you, but I would like to see you give him a chance. I've seen you with enough of the men you've dated to be able to guess why they never worked out. You never let down your guard with them. To be with someone, really be with someone, you need to let them in. I don't really care if you end up with Dylan, I just want to see you happy and with someone you trust enough to snort laugh in front of."

"I do not snort laugh."

"You do," Joanna said. "When you really let loose and laugh, something you don't let yourself do enough—not even with us."

Aly mulled their plan. "A hot tub test."

"So simple it's foolproof," Angelina said. "If he comes running out and dives in with you—take it from there."

"And if he doesn't?" Aly asked.

Neither of her friends had an answer for that.

Chapter Six

A SHORT TIME later Dylan was nursing a beer by the fireplace when Connor joined him. "Looks like everyone is calling it an early day," Connor said.

Dylan took a sip of his beer. "You too?"

Connor nodded. "Angelina's already in our room." He didn't move to leave, though. "You okay?"

"Yeah. I mean, I feel bad that I'm the reason everyone is here in the first place, but since I can't rewind time there's not much I can do with that."

"I called Dad. I wanted to make sure he knew we were safe."

Dylan groaned, but he understood. "How did he take it?"

"You know him, at first he kept thinking somehow we were responsible, but once he understood he just asked about how Bradford and Joanna were doing."

With a smile, Dylan said, "Can't really blame him. We certainly had our wild years."

Connor chuckled. "We did." His expression sobered. "When we thought we might also be in danger, you stepped right up and took control and I wasn't surprised. I talked to Angelina about that. You've always been there for me, Dylan. Always. I didn't realize how much I trust you to have my back."

"Mom asked me to look out for you."

"And you have. I love you."

"Shut the fuck up."

"No, let me say this. If today had gone differently, and we'd also been on someone's hit list, one of us might be dead tonight. I give you a lot of shit, but I don't want you to die before I tell you what a good brother you are. You're my best friend." He sighed. "I want you to have a life of your own, but I miss you."

Dylan put his beer aside and stood. "I needed time away to figure out a few things, but that doesn't mean I don't want to be part of your life." He'd never been one to gush his feelings, but if there'd ever been a day to do it, it was that day. "You're my best friend too. If I didn't love you, would I have sent all those ridiculous gifts?"

Connor pulled back the waistband of his jeans. "I'm wearing a pair now."

"I don't need to see which."

With a somber look in his eyes, Connor said, "I don't want to lose—this."

Unable to stand the tension of the moment, Dylan punched Connor in the arm as hard as he could. "Or this?"

Connor punched him back delivering an undercut just below the ribs, a move that doubled Dylan over. "More like this."

Rising up to his full height, Dylan prepared to sock his brother in the head, but Connor took off in a run and a chase ensued that knocked over several chairs and one small table. They eventually came to a winded, laughing stop near the front of the lodge.

"Hey," Connor asked, "is that Aly in the hot tub?"

Dylan whipped around. It was. All that was visible was her head, which was leaned back against a cushion, eyes closed. "Looks like it."

"All alone."

"And probably happy to be."

"Stop being such a pussy. Go join her. What's the worst that could happen?"

"She could try to drown me."

Connor laughed. "I had no idea you were such a coward, but I guess that's why I've always gotten laid more than you."

His brother's taunts didn't bother Dylan. That was their norm. What did bother him was how much he wanted to grab a pair of trunks and join Aly. He'd never been one to push himself on someone, though, and she'd given no indication that she wanted company. "I don't want to make her feel uncomfortable. No bathing suit, but I could go see if she's okay."

"Sure, because asking that naked will really put her at ease."

"You're an idiot."

Angelina chose that moment to appear behind Connor. Dylan could have warned him, but . . .

Connor puffed out his chest. "Maybe, but which one of us will be having sex tonight? Ask yourself that."

"You should ask yourself the same question," Angelina said, her hands going to her hips.

Connor was instantly at her side. "Aly's outside in the hot tub alone. I was just telling Dylan he should join her."

A smile twitched at Angelina's lips. "Mm-hmm."

A goofy smile lit Connor's face. "Okay, and maybe I was bragging." With that he swung Angelina up into his arms and twirled her around. "But how can I not when you make me so happy?"

When he stopped, Angelina was laughing. "Okay. Okay. You're making me dizzy."

Connor's response was a kiss.

Dylan's heart warmed. Especially after the day they'd had, it was good to see his brother so happy. "Good night, you two."

They didn't respond, but he wasn't expecting them to. They were still lost in each other when he turned to walk away.

He chose to put on a coat rather than bathing trunks before heading out to the hot tub. He'd meant what he'd said about not wanting to make her feel uncomfortable. He hated that he might have hurt her feelings earlier and wanted to clear that up. Everything else? There would be time to figure it out later.

THERE WERE WORSE things in the world than relaxing in a hot tub with a view of water on one side and mountains on the other. It would have been nice to also be beneath the stars, but that wouldn't happen until midnight.

It would also have been a huge ego boost if Dylan had instantly been at her side as soon as her tootsies had hit the water. That hadn't happened.

Aly was pragmatic by nature, or by habit, she wasn't sure which. She tipped her head back and closed her eyes, letting her mind wander. Nature versus nurture—it was a subject that fascinated some but one she hadn't spent much time thinking about. Her focus had always been on more concrete things. She'd studied mechanical engineering and computer science on the side because both helped her design better diagnostic tools. When a project required more than she knew, her knowledge in both areas at least gave her the ability to guide a team.

In her field she was known for being both innovative as well as demanding. She knew what she wanted and settled for nothing less, both from herself and from those she worked with. Some people applied nasty labels to her, but that wasn't uncommon for a strong woman.

Her patients saw another side of her. When they walked into her examination room each and every one of them was someone's daughter, wife, sister—mother. She treated all as if they were that in her life. Would she have brought that kind of compassion to her work if Joanna and Angelina had not come into her life? It was something she'd never know, but they'd both taught her so much about loyalty and acceptance, compassion and kindness. She didn't want to think about who she might have become without them.

That realization gave extra weight to Angelina's take on why Aly's relationships failed. *I do have a problem lowering my guard with men and I don't want that to always be the case.* It was what had brought her out to the hot tub. She'd conceded there was no way to know where things would go with Dylan, but the change needed to start within her. She needed to let someone in.

She'd imagined it going better than it had. To work, Dylan had to actually show up. She let herself fantasize what that might have been like. In her first fantasy he strolled up to the hot tub in just a towel, dropped it, and stepped into the water. She smiled. It would have been too much, but it sure was one hot vision.

Next she imagined him appearing beside the hot tub in swimming trunks and just standing there, giving her time to soak in the wide expanse of his chest and those deliciously muscled arms of his. "May I come in?" he asked in her imagination.

"You sure can," she purred.

He walked closer, his arousal tenting the front of his bathing trunks. "I do have one condition, though."

She answered in her mind. "Anything."

"Aly?"

He really did have the most incredible voice. She flicked her tongue across her lower lip and this time answered aloud in a husky tone, "Yes?"

"I saw you out here and hoped you wouldn't mind a little company."

Her eyes flew open and she sat forward with a flash and a

gasp. "Dylan!" She choked his name out like an accusation.

His smile was easy and a little apologetic. "I didn't mean to scare you."

"You didn't," she denied hotly as she fought to catch her breath. For just a second, fantasy and reality had mingled. She looked him over and disappointment flooded in. He was fully dressed, warm coat and all. It was hard to tell whether he'd come out to see if she was drowning or simply because he couldn't stay away.

She gave herself a stern mental shake. *He made what he feels and what he wants from me clear. I need to find a way to be okay with that.* "Sorry, you did surprise me. I was so relaxed I was almost sleeping." It was a lie, but close enough to the truth. She had been dreaming.

"I'm glad I came out, then. After a few drinks and the day we had, that would be dangerous. No one wants to fish you out of there in the morning."

His lecture was so far from what she'd imagined he'd say if he showed up that she growled, "Thanks, Dad, I'll keep that in mind."

Rather than being offended, he pulled up a wooden chair and settled into it. "I used to think you didn't like me, but I've decided you do—deep, deep down under all that bristle."

Bristle? That's far from sexy. Aly folded her arms across her chest beneath the water. *And not how I see myself.*

This time as she glared at him she asked herself where the anger was coming from. He'd done nothing wrong. In fact, he was being the friend he said he wanted to be. *I'm the problem.* "Sorry. And you're right, coming out here alone probably wasn't the wisest decision I've ever made." She started to rise to her feet.

He waved for her to sit back down. "Stay. I'm here now. Unless the water is too warm. If it's above one hundred degrees you shouldn't stay in too long."

She sat back beneath the water. "Not as warm as I hoped it would be." *In more ways than one.*

"That happens sometimes when you rent a place. No need to keep it high while the place is empty. Do you want me to turn it up?"

So logical. So nice. She wanted to smack him. "No, I'm fine."

He relaxed into his chair. "It's actually nicer at a lower temperature because you can stay in longer." He checked his watch. "We have a few hours until midnight or I'd suggest you hang out until the stars come out. We have this place for the week, though, so we can do this again."

This? Exactly this? With my luck, probably. "That would be nice."

After a pause, Dylan said, "I want to apologize for earlier. Clay is a good friend, but he can be—impulsive. I wanted to make sure he didn't go all "Fairy Godfather Extraordinaire" on us."

That made sense, especially considering how Dylan felt toward her. "I understand and really I'm okay."

He looked like he might say more on the subject, but didn't. Angelina's words echoed in her head. Dylan was her opportunity to be herself with a man, lower her walls, take a risk. They might never be more than friends, but Aly was beginning to understand what Angelina was asking her to do. She thought about the men she'd been with. None were still part of her life because none had ever made it past her defenses to become . . . a friend as well. She did want to learn how to let people in, and Dylan might be a good place to start. "Dylan."

"Yes?"

"I do want to be your friend."

His eyebrows rose and fell before he answered. "Okay."

She leaned back against the hot tub pillow again. Honesty was key to any friendship. "I've never had a male friend. Not a real one."

He cleared his throat. "I've had a lot of female friends, but lately they all want to fuck me and that complicates things."

For a second, she thought he was bragging, or coming on to her, but he looked sincere. She sat forward. "You're serious."

He hesitated as if choosing his words carefully. "My life changed dramatically in a short period of time. In some ways it's better, in some ways not so much. I'm still figuring it out."

There was a raw honesty to the moment. They'd touched on the subject before, but this time Aly felt comfortable sharing. "Career-wise I am exactly where I want to be, but when I step back and look at how I interact with people, I wish I could be more like Joanna. She's so open and optimistic."

Dylan nodded. "I can't tell you how many times I've wished I saw the world the way Connor does. I don't trust as easily, forgive as quickly, or walk as confidently into new social situations."

"That sounds like me."

"I told you we have more in common than you thought."

"We do." Aly searched his face. There was nothing there but warmth and acceptance, everything she'd been yearning for. Well, not quite everything, but the chance of having a real friendship with a man might just be worth suppressing what her body craved. "Tell me something I wouldn't know about you."

He scratched the back of his neck. "That's a tricky request. I'll do it if you do the same."

"Deal."

"My mother was sick for a very long time and Connor and I would act like idiots just to make her smile. Looking back, I'm not so sure Connor was acting."

Aly smiled at the joke.

Dylan continued, "Anyway, that became who we were. Even after she died, we clowned around. It was comfortable. When Viviana married Grant, Clay took me aside and told me I could be more. At first I didn't know what that meant, but I do now. I still like to laugh, and don't get me wrong, Connor and I were just beating the shit out of each other inside, but leaving my small town has changed my view of the world. I appreciate differences in people more than I did before. I even read for pleasure now."

"That's really good." Unable to resist, she added, "So if I looked on your phone it would be full of romance novels?"

"Some." He smiled. She liked that he had an easy way about him. He might not consider himself as confident as Connor, but that wasn't how she saw him. He took his time getting to know a situation before diving into it. That was smart. She did the same. He continued, "I'll read about almost anything, though. I can't see myself taking college courses like Connor is, but I like to know as much as I can about an area before I visit it. The more I travel, the more I enjoy learning about other cultures as well." After a pause, he added, "I really would like to show you Iceland. There are a handful of tourist spots that most people gravitate toward, but this country is about so much more."

"I'd like that." Joanna had said she wanted to stay and enjoy the house so there would be time.

"Your turn," he said.

"My . . . oh. What would someone probably not know about me?" She didn't open up to many so there was an ample amount she could choose from, but she wanted it to be something that mattered. "I've never had a pet."

"Really?" He looked surprised.

"Not even a goldfish."

"Why?"

She shrugged. "My father likes a quiet house."

"Goldfish don't make much noise."

"Pets are an unnecessary distraction and messy."

"I won't argue the messy part. My father recently adopted a Saint Bernard named Button. I'm pretty sure he gave him my old room."

Aly chuckled. "When I want to walk on the wild side I visit Joanna's rescue. I can't imagine cleaning up after all those animals on a daily basis, but she loves it. So does Bradford."

"When you care about something, cleaning up after it isn't such a big deal. Hell, you should see the destruction Connor leaves in his wake."

"I love that you're so close."

Dylan nodded. "Me too. Time away from him has helped me appreciate time with him more. No siblings?"

"No, I'm not even certain my father wanted me." Her joke fell flat and a short silence followed. "I love my father."

Bringing a hand to his chest, Dylan said, "Are you trying to convince me? Because I don't know him and I'm not doubting you."

His assertion made Aly face the truth—she was the one she was reassuring. "He and I are alike in many ways, but lately I'm wondering if I like some of what we have in common."

"Such as?"

This was the uncomfortable area where her defenses normally went up. She felt exposed and often that was when she got defensive. "Angelina says I have trouble letting people in."

"That's one of the things I like about you."

Aly's eyes widened then narrowed. "Really?"

His smile remained confident. "Absolutely, because when you finally admit you do like me, it'll mean something."

When I finally admit I like him? She looked away. *He doesn't mean that the way it sounds.* "I don't not like you."

Dylan barked out a laugh. "I don't not like you, either. What's a better basis for a friendship than that?"

She turned to look back at him and found herself smiling. "Sounds like a solid start to me."

After another lull in the conversation, she said, "I should probably head in."

He retrieved the terry cloth robe she'd brought out to the hot tub and held it up for her. She rose to her feet, a refreshing burst of cool air hit her skin and she rushed to meet him. Turning her back to him, she slid her arms in then spun to face him.

They were close, so much closer than she'd expected. Their eyes met. She tipped her head back, her lips slightly parted and for a moment there was nothing beyond him and the way he made her body hum.

His cheeks flushed. "You should get inside. It's cold out here."

She looked down, realizing only then that she hadn't yet closed the robe. Her nipples were at full attention, but not because of the cold. With a few swift moves, she secured the front of it and forced her feet to start toward the house. She left a wet path all the way to the door that he opened for her.

Just inside, they stood for a moment, simply looking into each other's eyes again. Aly could have sworn he felt something too. How could an attraction be so strong and not be mutual?

She swallowed hard. "Thank you for coming out to check on me."

"Anytime."

"Good night, Dylan."

He dipped his head as if he might kiss her, then said near her ear, "Good night, Aly," and walked away.

Chapter Seven

DYLAN WOKE BEFORE the rest of the house to go for his daily run. Early sunlight was the perk of summer in the Westfjords. His workout normally consisted of cardio then lifting every other day.

Prior to working with a personal trainer during *Danger Doubled*, he'd stayed fit by lifting heavy shit and carrying it around. In high school, he'd spent time in the weight room, but working for his father had built up more of his bulk muscle.

He smiled as he remembered the first trainer who had been assigned to him. She'd asked him if he understood the difference between eccentric and concentric movements as well as the importance of managing metabolic stress. After sitting through a lengthy explanation of each as well as a detailed plan that included exact times for each activity, Dylan had removed his shirt and flexed.

She'd blushed and told him to continue doing whatever his current workout was. He'd laughed and done just that.

Stripping off his shirt had been a joke and back then Claire had still been spit-shining his transformation from rowdy redneck to Hollywood heartthrob. Her words, not his. He was now fully aware that not all of his small-town humor translated well in "sophisticated" circles.

As he ran, his thoughts returned to Aly the night before. *Friends?* Who had come up with that stupid idea? *Oh, yes: me.*

He hadn't expected to go from constantly being irritated by her to having a hard time thinking about anything beyond her. The sight of her in a tiny blue bikini surfacing from the hot tub and walking toward him, dripping wet and pink was still painfully vivid. Painful because just the thought of it gave him an erection and no man liked to run with one.

Was she attracted to him as well? He couldn't tell. There were times when he would have bet his life she was, but then she said or did something that made him less certain. The last thing he wanted to do was make a move on her, discover it was unwelcome, and make things awkward between them.

Truth was, the more they spoke, the more he was beginning to like Aly. She had a softer side, one she reserved for those closest to her. She'd said she'd never had a real male friend. He found that interesting.

And who the hell has never had a pet?

Or, more precisely, what kind of parent doesn't even let their child have a goldfish?

His heart had hurt for her when she'd joked that she wasn't certain her father had even wanted her. Somewhere under all that confidence was a doubt that no child should have. When Dylan thought about all the stupid things he'd ever done, all the times his father had lectured him on his behavior—never, not even once, had he ever doubted his father's love.

She'd also said he held himself to the same high standards he'd held her to. That didn't sound like a place where mistakes were tolerated and what child doesn't make them? It sounded like she was figuring out who she was away from her father. He understood that more than she'd probably ever know.

After pausing to check the time, Dylan decided to head back. When they'd spoken about it the day before it had seemed like everyone wanted to do their own thing. He wanted to get out into the world on his day off.

With Aly.

He kept his pace steady and went over several possible outings he could suggest to her. Was she the type who would want to visit a sorcerer's cottage, explore one of the towns, hike to a waterfall, sail, simply tour around by car? He had no idea but he was looking forward to seeing the country through her eyes.

Through her eyes.

I know what she'd like to do, and I bet I know someone who knows someone who could make that happen.

The house was still quiet when he returned to it. He showered, dressed, and sat down with his phone. By the time he heard Aly rustling around in their shared bathroom, he'd already made several calls and was feeling good about his decision.

It wasn't a romantic outing. It wasn't meant to be.

Friendships were about more.

The sound of her turning on the shower had him scrambling to gather his things and vacate his room. It was bad enough that he couldn't shake the image of her in a bathing suit, he didn't need to imagine her in less.

ALY WAS APPLYING mascara when there was a knock on her bedroom door. Could it be Dylan? Possibly. Either way, most things were better faced head-on. "Come in." After the sound of the outer door opening she said, "I'm in the bathroom finishing up getting ready, but I'm dressed."

She was both a little disappointed and a little relieved when it was Angelina and Joanna who popped into view. Angelina started with, "So, tell us everything. Connor said Dylan went out to see you."

The doctor in Aly was concerned by the dark circles she saw beneath Joanna's eyes, the friend in her wanted to hug her and let her cry. "More importantly, how are you holding up? You didn't sleep at all last night, did you?"

"I couldn't stop reliving the moment when I thought Bradford might be dead. You'd think the scariest part would have been the fight for the gun, but it wasn't. When I found the caretaker dead and saw the drag marks beyond him— that's the moment that haunts me." Joanna shook her head as if trying to shake those images free.

"Because you felt powerless."

"Yes." She hugged her arms around herself. "The fight actually felt good. The other thing I can't shake is knowing I'm capable of murder."

Aly leaned a hip against the sink counter and let out a slow breath. "I read an article once about a man in Laos who never wanted to be a soldier. He was a peaceful man, a shaman. When war came, he swore he would save lives on both sides. War came closer and people in the villages he'd been to were killed—and he clung to the belief that he would bring only good if it came closer. Then people he knew began to die, and not by the hand of Americans, and he learned to shoot a rifle. War is an ugly thing that plays by its own rules. By the time they came for his village, for his family, he'd lost count of the number of lives he'd taken. He was able to escape Laos and take his wife and children to the United States, but that experience cost him. It took him thirty years to put enough distance between himself and that time to be able to write about it. He said you don't know who you are until someone comes for your family. You don't want to know."

"That's how I feel. I want to go back to believing I don't have that side." Joanna's eyes filled with tears. "It must be how Bradford feels. That's why he stopped me."

"Do you know what that man did in the United States? He became a shaman again and said everything he'd learned about himself helped him counsel others. He didn't feel better than anyone else and that allowed him to reach those who could see no good in themselves. Everything you went through here, I have to believe will give you even more empathy for those horses you save."

Joanna nodded and released a shaky breath. "I had no idea you were so good at treating something above the waist."

Aly laughed, Angelina joined in. The joke released some of the tension in the air.

After reaching for a tissue and dabbing at the corners of her eyes, Joanna said, "Don't think this gets you out of telling us about Dylan. In fact, hearing about him is the kind of distraction I need."

Aly glanced at the door behind her, the one that opened to Dylan's bedroom.

"Don't worry," Angelina said, "he's already having breakfast with everyone. That's how we knew it was safe to come and grill you."

Turning her attention back to her reflection, Aly gave her hair a final brush through. "So he did come out to see me at the hot tub, but nothing happened. He stayed fully clothed and we just talked."

"Talking is good," Joanna said.

Aly began to tie back her hair in a loose braid. "And we're moving ahead as friends."

"I like that," Angelina said. "So, did you make plans for today?"

"He said he'd like to show me Iceland, the side he has gotten to know. I can do that or I can go wherever you both are going."

Joanna raised and lowered her shoulders. "Bradford and I decided we need a quiet day. We thought we'd do a little hiking, maybe stop somewhere for a drink . . . just the two of us. He's still shaken from yesterday, but he's here and said he'd like to go forward with the vacation, so that's huge."

Angelina wrinkled her nose. "Connor found a Viking-themed adventure cruise. You dress like a Viking, drink, pillage. I'm not really sure, but he said it sounded fun and I could use a good laugh. You could join us if you want."

"That's okay." She groaned inwardly and hoped that wasn't what Dylan was also going to ask her to do.

Angelina added, "I'm pretty sure Clay and Lexi said they wanted to hunt down Helka and her friends to see where they live and what they might need. Ian and Claire offered to join them, but probably to keep them in check."

"Oh, Clay," Aly said with humor. "No, I can't say that's how I'd like to spend the day either."

"What do you want to do?" Joanna asked.

Angelina chuckled. "She wants to *do* Dylan, but I'm sure she'd settle for spending the day with him."

Aly laughed as well. "Stop. You're not far from the truth, but we're not going there, remember?" She rubbed a hand across her forehead. "I'll see what Dylan wants to do—unless he also wants to be a Viking today. I don't want him that badly."

Angelina rolled her eyes. "Don't knock it until you try it. Before Connor I would have said the same, but he makes everything fun. Plus, seeing him happy makes me happy, even if it means I'll be swigging ale and . . . I don't really know what a Viking adventure cruise entails, but it'll be an experience."

Joanna rubbed her hands over her eyes as if trying once again to clear her thoughts, then said, "Let's go see what Dylan came up with. It's kind of fun not having any idea what he'd suggest."

"Yes," Aly answered, but thought: *Fun? More like scary. I half hope it'll be something so horrible it'll shake me free from his spell.* She shook her head and waved for her friends to lead the way out of her bedroom. In a heartbeat they were joining the rest of the group at a long table where some were already eating breakfast. Dylan was standing off to the side looking freshly showered and even better than he had the night before. How was that possible? The man had a glow to him and the smile he shot her nearly melted her to a puddle of need right there.

He crossed the room to join her. "Hope I wasn't too noisy this morning. I headed out early for a run."

That explained the color on his cheeks. "I rolled over, dragged the blanket up over my head, then rolled over again. Does that count for exercise?"

He chuckled. "A lot of things count."

Her eyebrows rose as she read into his claim, then she decided he hadn't meant his words the way she'd taken them. Just when she decided he was innocent and she had a filthy mind, he winked and her cheeks warmed.

He leaned in and said, "I'm sorry, it's just so easy to rile you."

Her chin rose and she held back her first defensive retort. Seriously, if she couldn't stop overreacting around him they'd never actually become friends. She conceded with a smile. "Cute."

Still standing close enough to have her heart racing, he flexed his shoulders and said, "I think the description you're looking for is strikingly handsome and witty, but somehow still approachable."

Her smile widened. "It's like you can read my mind." *Friends.* She told herself, *I can do this.* "Last night you mentioned you'd like to show me around Iceland. If you're still—"

"I have the whole day planned."

"You do?" Her eyes rounded.

"I can tell you or I can surprise you."

Without missing a beat, she said, "I'm always better if I know ahead of time." She'd never enjoyed surprises.

"Good to know." He waved toward a table of breakfast foods. "Grab something to eat, meet me at the table, and I'll lay out what I have planned." He paused and his forehead furrowed. "I think you'll like it, but nothing is set in stone. We can change any or all of it."

She searched his face. What would a man like Dylan plan as an outing? She really had no idea. She would have said she was in for whatever, but if it was something wilder than one of Connor's ideas she wasn't sure she would be. "Thank you."

He nodded then walked over to sit with the group at the table. As she filled her plate, she kept glancing over at him. He was dressed casually in black jeans, a nice shirt and jacket. His shoes looked like a fit for walking but not hiking. Interesting. She was glad she'd chosen a simple woolen sweater and slacks rather than jeans.

At the table, Dylan was sitting between Clay and Connor. The open seat was between Lexi and Angelina across from them. It made her wish she'd pushed for the details of the day while there hadn't been an audience. She didn't want to embarrass Dylan, so if they were doing something she wouldn't feel comfortable doing she'd agree to it then but take him aside at the first opportunity. She greeted everyone as she sat down then accepted a hot coffee from one of the house staff.

Aly's fork hadn't made it to her mouth yet when Clay asked, "Did I hear that you and Dylan are heading off on your own today?"

Meeting trouble head-on, Aly said, "We are."

"And that you let him plan the day?"

"I did."

Clay smiled. "I offered to help, but Dylan said he is 'all set.' I can't wait to hear what he came up with."

Me too.

"Knock it off, Clay," Dylan said lightly. He and Clay were a pair Aly wouldn't have expected to become friends, but each time she saw them together it made sense. Dylan was blunt, without being angry. He was grateful without fawning over Clay. In fact, the more Aly thought about it, the more she liked how down-to-earth Dylan still was. *At least, here, away from fans.*

Angelina piped in, "I'll admit I'm curious as well."

"Hell, even I am," Ian joked from across the table. "Aly, I hope you're prepared for whatever."

Dylan shook his head, but he was smiling. "You're all making this into a bigger deal than it is. I offered to show Aly around and that's all this is. A tour, just like I offered the rest of you losers, but you wanted to go off on your own."

Connor punched Dylan in the shoulder. "I still can't believe you passed on the Viking adventure."

Clay looked back and forth between Aly and Dylan. "That's not really Aly's style. Nor is an all-day hike. No offense Aly."

What the fuck? Aly looked down at her body. She might not exercise, but she was physically fit. "Only a little taken."

Lexi intervened, "Clay, not everyone gets your humor."

With a shrug, Clay said, "I wasn't passing judgment. I just thought a doctor would be more into exercise."

"I work," Aly said in a curt tone, "a lot. Try it, then see how much time you have to work out."

Dylan coughed and looked as if he were holding back a laugh. Clay opened his mouth to say something back, but Dylan put up a hand. "Ding. Ding. Ding. Round one goes to the doctor. Clay, it's breakfast and Aly hasn't had her coffee yet. Do you want to tangle with her or do you want to hear about the day I have planned?"

"I have no desire to *tangle* with anyone especially so early in the day." With a tip of his head, Clay said, "My apologies, Aly." He leaned over to hug Lexi. "As my wife says, my humor is an acquired taste."

Aly was tempted to tell Dylan she was perfectly capable of dealing with Clay on her own, but it was nice to have him in her corner. She also appreciated how casually he'd handled the situation. Clay didn't look at all upset and what could have been a tense moment wasn't. *It's a skill I wish I were better at.* She'd been raised to believe the direct route was always the best, but there was merit to a softer touch. "Your humor is one of the many things I love about you, Clay." She raised her coffee. "And I really can't be counted on to be human until I've finished at least one cup."

Joanna raised her cup in solidarity. "Amen."

Clay sat back in his seat, turning his attention to Dylan. "Don't worry, Aly, if I'm put off at all it's by Dylan's lack of interest in my services. Even Bradford—"

"Enough, Clay," Bradford spoke up with a force that brought conversation all around the table to a halt. The silence was prolonged and heavy.

"So moody." Eventually Clay said, "It's been almost twenty-four hours since your abduction, Bradford. How long do you plan to milk it?"

No one spoke.

No one dared look toward Bradford.

After a moment, he started to laugh. "Fucking Clay."

Others joined in and the tension left the group. Lexi gave Clay's arm a playful smack. "Oh, hon."

Across the table Aly met Dylan's gaze. His smile froze. For a moment Aly felt connected to him in a way she couldn't explain. Her rational mind attempted to quantify or justify it, but couldn't. The feeling simply was. She cleared her throat. "So, Dylan, are you ever going to tell me what you came up with for today?"

Continuing to hold her gaze, he said, "I hired a helicopter to take us to a teaching hospital located in Akureyri where the CEO promised to give us a tour tailored to your interests. He's aware of you and your work, so he arranged for you to also meet the hospital's liaison to the National Medical Invention Association."

It wasn't often that Aly was left speechless but her jaw went slack and she just looked at him. How was it that the man she kept thinking was all wrong for her had come up with a day that sounded so right?

At her lack of response, he rushed to add, "If that sounds too much like work while you're on vacation, I can cancel and we can fly off to Reykjavik. We have the helicopter all day so we can go anywhere and do anything."

"No, it's fine," she said breathlessly. Still processing what he'd done, she asked, "How did you set all that up?"

His confident smile returned and he shrugged one muscled shoulder. "Well, I *am* Dylan Sutton."

Across the table, Connor made a sound akin to a puppy growl. "Angelina, you don't want to go on a tour of some business or something, do you? I can cancel the Viking adventure."

Angelina walked around the table and slid her arms around his neck from behind. "Don't you dare." She leaned around and kissed his cheek. "I've been practicing my pillaging face all morning."

His smile returned and, with a twist and one strong move, he settled her across his lap. "I just want you to know that I would plan a long and boring day too, because your happiness matters to me."

Angelina laughed. "If I was looking for boring I wouldn't be marrying you, Sweet Cheeks." That gained her a kiss from Connor.

Seeing Angelina with him would never get old for Aly. After watching her friend struggle for so many years, it was amazing to see her so comfortable with herself and happy. Aly looked across at Dylan. His expression had turned puzzled.

He turned to Clay and asked, "Do you think a hospital tour sounds boring?"

Clay shrugged. "Yes, but I'm not the one you should ask."

All eyes turned to Aly. In general she was a private person. She chose her words carefully, trying to honor what Dylan needed to hear with what she felt comfortable sharing. "I love everything about it. Thank you, Dylan. It's more than I ever expected."

His smile returned. "I'm glad. We leave right after breakfast."

Conversation started around the table again and Aly gulped down some of her coffee. Her stomach was churning from nerves so she forced down a few bites of toast as well. She reminded herself that her outing with Dylan was not a date. It might be the single most considerate day planned by anyone she'd ever been with, but she needed to remember that she wasn't *with* him.

This is what friends do—they listen and go out of their way to make each other happy.

How could something so good also make her a little sad? *I've always been a strictly realistic person. Why can't I be with Dylan?*

I need to find a way for this to be enough.

Chapter Eight

SEVERAL HOURS LATER Dylan and Aly stepped out onto a helipad, waving at the gathered hospital staff. It hadn't been a swashbuckling wild time, but Aly hadn't stopped smiling since they'd entered the building and that was what mattered most to Dylan.

The pilot opened a door to the helicopter and helped Aly into the private cabin first. As soon as the door closed behind Dylan, the noise from the spinning blades above diminished significantly. Aly secured herself into the seat next to him. "What an amazing day, thank you so much."

Her smile did funny things to his ability to breathe. "You're welcome. How did it feel to realize they were all aware of the work you're doing?"

"Wonderful. Crazy. I was prepared for some criticism since Iceland is ranked third in the world on Bloomberg Healthiest Country Index, but they seemed to understand the complexity of the challenges doctors face in the United States."

"I liked how they were honest about the issues that arise with universal health care as well. It was an interesting discussion to listen in on."

She gave him a long look. "You weren't bored?"

He could have lied and said every moment of it had been fascinating, but decided to be honest instead. "It had its moments. My favorite part was when the head of the invention association asked if you'd look over some prototypes and give your feedback. That's when it got really interesting for me."

"Me too," she said with a vigorous nod. "What did you think of the pocket ultrasound?"

"I couldn't understand why they hadn't thought of them being compatible with smartphones. That was a great suggestion."

"I loved your idea of making them multi-purpose with attachments. Also, when she mentioned the potential of do-it-yourself vaginal ultrasounds, your comment about how that might be a comfort to women going through in vitro fertilization was spot-on."

"A woman in our film crew is trying to get pregnant and she talks to me about it sometimes. A lot of injections and doctor visits to check if her eggs are maturing. Sometimes it's two or more visits a week to make sure it's working. That's a lot of stress on her. I was just thinking that something like a pocket ultrasound linked to her phone would let her send updates to her doctor without having to miss so much time at work. It's not fair, but some directors are dicks and hold that kind of thing against a woman."

"Isn't that illegal?"

"Only if people can prove it. It's one of those unspoken

things that everyone knows happens but no one fights because everyone wants to work. I can't change the world, but Clay has helped me hook up with directors who are known for non-discriminatory practices across the board. I wouldn't want to work with any other kind."

"Me neither."

The helicopter tilted as it took off. Aly gasped from the surprise of it and grasped Dylan's forearm. He laid his hand over hers. "You okay?"

She slid her hand out from under his. "Sorry. I actually like to fly, but when it tilts—"

He frowned. "It's okay to need someone now and then, Aly. Centipedes scare the shit out of me. All those legs." He shuddered. "I had one crawl on my neck once and I don't think I've been right since."

"Did Connor save you?" That smile had been his goal. She needed to do it more.

"Save? Laugh his ass off while I had a meltdown—same thing, right?"

"Sure."

The pilot came over the intercom and asked if they wanted to stop at a geothermal pool for a dip on the way back. "We didn't bring bathing suits," Dylan said.

"I know of a secluded one if you're interested anyway. You wouldn't be the first to strip and dip."

Nudity didn't embarrass Dylan. To fully enjoy Iceland and all its nature had to offer, one had to let go of one's inhibitions. "Aly?"

Her eyes were wide. "Yes?"

"It's up to you. I've done it before and it's really not a big deal, but I completely understand if you're not comfortable."

There was a long pause after which he was positive she would admit she wasn't. Instead her chin rose and she said, "I'd love to try it."

Holy shit.

That's all.

Just—holy shit.

DECLINING THE OFFER had come to mind, but the talk Aly had had with the Icelandic men regarding nudity was still echoing in her thoughts. *I'm a doctor. Bodies are what I do. Any shame I have about my own has been learned and can be shed.*

There is nothing inherently sexual about an unclothed body.

If my goal is to lower my guard with a man—really, could there be a more direct way?

Dylan dipped his head forward to meet her gaze. "You don't have to do this."

"I want to."

He made a face and nodded toward her hand which was clenching the armrest of her chair. She released her death grip on it, flexed her fingers and took a deep, calming breath. Images of how he might look naked swept in but she pushed them back. This wasn't about that. What had Clay told him he could be? More? That's what she wanted to become—not different, just more than she'd allowed herself to be in the past.

More confident.

More daring.

In a tone that sounded tense to even her own ears, she said, "I need to do this."

His expression appeared conflicted. "If you want to go in on your own, I can stay with the pilot."

"Did you go in alone?"

"No, a bunch of us from the movie joined this German group that came in to do some CGI work. It was a fun time."

"Like orgy-fun or like volleyball-naked fun?"

He coughed. "I don't know how wild you think I am but I'm a one partner at a time kind of guy. A group of us heard of a place that was nearby, we all took showers, dove in, drank some beer, told some hilarious stories, grabbed our clothes and went home."

"Men and women?"

"Yes."

She folded her arms across her chest. "So it doesn't *have* to be a sexual thing."

He swallowed visibly. "It wasn't that day."

"Then I can do this." Nodding, Dylan was suddenly the one who appeared tense. She was torn between being determined to do this and feeling like she was ruining the experience for him. Lowering her arms, she said, "Unless you don't want to."

"I'm fine with it." His tone was higher than normal. He cleared his throat. "After you've been here awhile it's really nothing."

The pilot came back on and said, "We will be landing

near my uncle's farm house. The geo pool is a short walk from there, but he is strict about who goes in it and that they clean off first. Due to tourists many natural pools have too much bacteria in them to be used. We don't get as many tourists as you'd see in Southern Iceland, but still not all have been as respectful of the land as a local would be. Leave it the way you found it is the best motto if you want to be welcome in these parts. My uncle tests the water on a regular basis and it's clean, but he has a bathing house set up beside it with towels you can borrow in return for a favor."

"A favor?" Dylan asked, exchanging a look with Aly.

"He bought a drone to help him find his sheep in the mountains. If you'd like to use his towels, he said you can if you stay for a quick meal and a demonstration."

Aly nodded. It sounded like the perfect way to round off their day.

"Tell your uncle we would love that. Had I known we would be visiting your family I would have brought a gift," Dylan said.

"Don't worry, I brought a bottle of his favorite vodka. My uncle normally doesn't like international guests, but Freyja is my cousin and she said Anna and Margret had only good things to say about you."

Throwing his hands up in the air, Dylan laughed. "Even you? I make one mistake . . ."

"Or two to be more precise." The pilot was laughing as well. "You're in the wrong part of the country if you were hoping for anonymity."

"A little too late to tell me that *now*," Dylan joked.

There was nothing appealing about imagining Dylan with another woman, but Aly had to admit it was entertaining to see how the news had traveled. It was also fascinating to Aly that far from being a scandal it was becoming more of a community wide private joke—one that didn't seem to bother even Dylan.

Because not everything in life is a tragedy.
Or as serious as my father makes it out to be.

Dylan bent near her ear and joked, "It's not nice to find so much amusement in my misfortune."

It was then she realized she was grinning from ear to ear. "I never claimed to be nice." The look they shared turned heated, at least on her side, so she turned her attention back to the window.

The helicopter dipped to the side and the pilot said, "I can't do a full flyover because my uncle will kill me if I send his sheep scattering. But if you look out the window on your right you will see the two pools. They are both hot spring fed. The small round one surrounded by rocks has been used by my family for centuries. It's deep enough to go into and sit. The large blue cement pool next to it is what our family uses the most. If it gets too hot there is a hose with water from a stream that can help regulate it. You're welcome to use either, or both."

To Aly they looked much more out in the open than she'd expected. Was a hedge or a little privacy fence too much to ask for? She released a shaky breath. *Being confidently out in the open with nature is the point.*

"You still good?" Dylan asked from just behind her.

Without looking back at him, she answered, "Absolutely."

They landed in a field beside a stone path that led to a simple rectangular house with several barns behind. After a brisk walk to the house, the pilot introduced them to his uncle who didn't look nearly as old as Aly had expected. He welcomed them inside and offered them a hot beverage.

Aly declined. She wanted to get the whole naked pool thing done and over.

Dylan declined as well, but began to ask the farmer questions. So many questions. How long had he lived there? Was the land attached to his father's farm? How many of the local farms were still in operation? Were there any fishermen in the family? Were any of the locals on the national handball team?

At first Aly thought Dylan might be making the farmer uncomfortable, but right before her eyes she saw a connection form. The man asked Dylan about his own family, how he'd gotten into the movie business and if he already had his next movie deal lined up. Dylan answered each question with an open honesty that warmed Aly's heart. This was how strangers became friends. It was real. Why wasn't there more of this in her life?

When the farmer asked her about her job she found herself answering in the same open manner Dylan had. She told him about the academic town she'd grown up in, how her career was currently all consuming, but how she was trying to bring balance back to her life. She also shared some of her experience from the hospital tour that morning.

It was hard to tell if the farmer was impressed or not. As soon as she stopped talking, he asked, "Would you like to see my drone?"

"We'd love to," Aly answered for both Dylan and herself.

The pilot stayed inside while his uncle led them outside. The monitor in the farmer's hand was large enough that they could both share the view once his drone hit the air. Aly hadn't expected to enjoy the experience as much as she did. As he gave them an aerial tour of the area, he also told a story of twenty or so feral sheep that had recently been located in the mountains with a similar drone. He spoke of a difficult hike to get to an area in the mountains that dipped down enough to allow for grass to grow and provided just enough shelter for the sheep to survive the harsh winters. "Centuries of raising sheep and the hardiest and largest I have seen in my life are the ones we brought down from the mountain."

"That's so interesting. Do you think they cross bred with something?" Aly asked.

The farmer scratched his chin and looked at the mountain in the distance. "More likely the weak died and the strongest bred. Plus the field up there has remained untouched by our herds, so it's lush. I call their size proof of the healing power of nature. In trying to make everything better, we often do too much. Sometimes the best thing we can do for nature is to leave it alone."

"I wholeheartedly agree," Dylan said.

Aly nodded.

"Well, let's get you into that pool you came for. On a scale of one to ten how shy would you say you two are?"

Not knowing what the scale was in reference to, Aly had a difficult time answering that.

Dylan said, "About a five."

The farmer nodded and landed his drone before leading them back to pools. He gave them quick instructions on the necessity to wash down well before entering either.

"Thank you," Dylan said and shook his hand.

Aly did the same.

"I'll put some fish soup on," the farmer said. "You'll be hungry after your swim so come on up to the house when you're ready."

Neither Aly nor Dylan spoke during the walk to the shower house. Just outside of it, Dylan said, "My guess is there's only one stall. Do you want to go first or second?"

"Second?" Aly said, fighting back a mild panic.

Dylan headed in. The sound of water running followed. Some singing. She smiled. Really?

When he emerged, he had a towel wrapped around his waist and that was it. "The water is instantly warm. Must be spring fed as well. There's soap. I'm thinking we should start in the large pool, maybe get some laps in."

"Sounds good," Aly croaked.

As he walked away, he whipped the towel off and tossed it on a chair beside the large pool. Aly swayed on her feet. He was perfection. She told herself to look away, but there were few moments in her life that had ever been as vivid.

Just before he dove in he looked back over his shoulder and waved. She blushed straight down to her toes. Without fanfare he began to do laps, those powerful back muscles of his flexing with each stroke. She just stood there, mouth open.

"It's beautiful," he called out.

It sure is.

She forced her feet to carry her inside the shower house. It was rustic, but clean. There was only one shower area with several showerheads and an area off to the side for clothing to be hung. She stripped down, washed off and wrapped a towel securely around herself.

At the edge of the pool she hesitated. Dylan was swimming, respectfully not looking over. She placed her towel on a chair beside his and cool air blew across her still damp bare skin like a kiss from nature. She shivered and quickly slipped beneath the water.

The water was hot and clear. Dylan's face was pink, likely from the temperature. She moved farther into the pool and started to swim as if she were alone.

Dylan swam up to the side of her. "Are you up for a race?"

Her entire body went into some kind of overload and she had to put her feet on the bottom of the pool for a moment. "Race?"

"Sure, unless you're certain I'd win. I mean, I'm a good swimmer. If you're not, I don't want to embarrass you."

Aly put a hand on her hip beneath the water. "What makes you think I'm not an amazing swimmer?"

"Are you?"

"I was on a high school team."

His eyebrows rose. "Then we go to that wall and the ladder and I won't feel bad when I kick your ass." He took off with a dive.

Nudity forgotten, she followed him and fell into the efficient pace she'd often used in the past. Winning in a sport had never held much value to her, which had always driven her swim coach a little mad. It had been important to her father that her education was well-rounded and looking back, it had been his idea that she join the team. Had she ever enjoyed it? The thought that she hadn't allowed herself to ask that question earlier gave her strokes more power. She reached the wall just before Dylan and spun under, pushing off it first. She surfaced near the ladder a mere second or two before Dylan.

He shook the water from his hair, then gave her a look. "You don't look happy."

"I am," she growled.

He frowned, curling his mouth down and said, "This is how I look when I'm angry." Then he smiled. "This is me happy." Frowned again. "Sad or upset." Smiled again. "Happy."

Her mood lightened. "Sorry. I was just thinking about something completely irrelevant."

"Want to talk about it?"

"Do men really ask that?"

"Oh, oh, look who is the closet sexist. Under all this muscle, I'm just a person. I worry about shit. Sometimes I even cry."

She searched his face and found nothing but open friendship. "I don't—cry that is. A tear or two here and there, sure, but not full on cry. I understand the cathartic value of it, but I"—she searched within herself for the source of why—"I can't."

"Because it's a waste of time."

"I guess." She let out a breath. "Maybe I feel a little self-conscious too. Even when I'm alone."

"Your father sure did a job on you." When she opened her mouth to deny it, he added, "I know you love him, but the man could have given you a little more room to be you."

There was light sarcasm in his tone, but worse, he was right. Aly swam off to put a little distance between herself and what she didn't want to think about.

He followed her, not close enough to make her feel awkward, but keeping pace with her. When she stopped, he said, "Sorry."

"Me too. I feel like I'm constantly apologizing to you."

He smiled. "You are, but it's kind of cute."

"I'm anything but *cute.*"

The sound of cars pulling in cut off whatever Dylan might have responded. Aly swam to the edge of the pool. Two cars, seemingly brimming with people pulled up and parked beside the shower building. "Oh, my God, who are those people?"

Beside her, Dylan said, "We can bolt for our clothes if we hurry."

"It's too late for that." The passengers of the car piled out. Men and women varying in ages from their mid-twenties to a few women who looked like they might be in their eighties.

The pilot came rushing down the path pausing to greet several members of the group. He had an apologetic smile as he approached the pool. "My uncle might have told the family that you would be here. They love company."

His uncle appeared beside him. "You did say you were comfortable."

An older woman made her way to the side of the pool. "What a charming couple. Do you mind if we join you?" She pulled out a bathing suit from her bag. "We all brought suits so you wouldn't feel uncomfortable."

"*You* brought suits so *we* don't feel uncomfortable?" Aly asked, and her embarrassment over the situation was replaced by amusement. She turned to Dylan, barely containing a laugh. "*She's* going to wear a suit so *we* feel more comfortable."

He smiled. "It's very thoughtful actually."

Aly started to laugh.

Dylan joined in.

Giving in the sheer absurdity of the situation, Aly laughed so hard she snorted, which only made her laugh more.

"Have they been drinking?" the older woman asked. "I don't understand what's so funny."

The pilot responded, "Americans. No one fully understands their humor."

Another older woman joined the group. "Are they okay with company?"

"Who can tell?" the first woman grumbled.

Aly calmed enough to say, "I'm sorry. Yes, come on in.

We're grateful to your family for sharing the pool with us."

The women said something to each other in Icelandic, then called to the others and they began piling into the shower house, first the women then the men. The farmer returned to the house, after saying he would put more soup on. People began to emerge in bathing suits from the shower building and climb into the large pool.

At first Aly pretended she was clothed. If she didn't look down, she could. As the group came closer it was sheer grit that kept her from bolting. Eventually, though, as conversation began to flow, she relaxed.

What unfolded was a larger version of the conversation Dylan had had with the farmer when they'd first arrived. They asked Aly and Dylan about their lives in the United States. They told them about their own lives. It was comfortable, friendly and pure.

By the time the farmer returned and said the soup was ready, Aly had relaxed enough to regret that the experience was coming to an end. In that pool she felt as if she'd shed all the inhibitions and restrictive expectations that weighed her down normally. She felt lighter, freer—as if she'd glimpsed a version of who she might have been.

I don't have to become more—I am more.

Dylan stepped out of the pool and wrapped a towel around himself then held one out for her. She walked toward him, this time confident in her nudity. She turned, allowing him to drape it over her shoulders then headed into the shower while he waited outside. Some women were in there already in various stages of washing off or getting dressed.

She chatted with them easily.

When she emerged, Dylan said, "You look happy."

She smiled up at him. "I am. This is probably the single best day of my life. Thank you."

His eyes darkened and he looked about to say something, but instead turned, dropped his towel, and dove back into the water. She worried for a moment that she might have upset him, then decided he was probably just cold and realized why the men were lingering in the pool rather than cueing up for their turn in the shower.

THE MEAL THAT followed their swim reminded Dylan of everything he missed about the town he'd grown up in. Out of courtesy for them, the conversation remained in English, but it flowed easily with enough laughter and teasing to make it feel like home.

It was wonderful enough to make a man feel guilty for the battle he was fighting with arousal. He was flanked by women three times his age and reviewing the last decade of football stats in his head was all that stood between him and an erection. Hot water wasn't as effective as cold for what he'd required after Aly had walked over to him naked and looked up at him like she was his, but it had helped. The cold shower that he'd followed it with as well as distance from her had solved his issue, at least temporarily.

He remembered Connor once telling him that he couldn't imagine being with another woman after he met Angelina. Dylan had thought he was exaggerating, but Aly was setting up camp in his head and his pants. She looked up from talking to the farmer and smiled. He nearly missed his mouth with his spoon.

The older woman on his right said, "Young love is a beautiful thing."

He placed his spoon on the plate beside his bowl. "We're just friends."

She lowered her voice and said, "That never stopped me from having sex with someone."

Dylan started choking and reached for a glass of water.

She put a hand on his arm. "I should warn you, I've always been the town flirt."

He could see why. Despite her age, she was fit from a lifetime of being outdoors and active. Her features were classically beautiful and her eyes were full of mischief. He'd bet she'd broken her share of hearts along the way. "I'm sure you still have a line of admirers."

Her eyes lit with humor. "I do." Her expression turned more serious. "None I look at the way you look at her. I only felt that way about one man and that was a long time ago."

"I don't—" He stopped. He didn't really know what he felt.

As if she could hear his thoughts, she said, "It's okay to not know. It's okay to get it wrong before you get it right. Just remember to savor the journey. If I could go back, I would have worried less about where it was going and spent more time enjoying getting there."

He placed his hand over hers and bent near her ear to say, "She's clear about what she wants from me and that's a friend."

The woman gave his forearm a squeeze and smiled. "Then that's where you start. Be patient."

I can do that.

Lowering his voice, he said, "It'd be a hell of a lot easier if she kept her clothes on."

That sent the woman next to him into a fit of laughter. The woman on his other side asked something in Icelandic. The response she received sent a wave of laughter around the table.

Aly's eyebrows came together, forming that slight crease in her forehead. She looked across at Dylan with a clear question in her eyes that he pretended he didn't have an answer for. No one seemed to be laughing at them—rather they seemed to be hoping it worked out for them. He was beginning to hope the same thing.

Conversation returned to English and the moment passed. After dinner, the farmer brought out a bottle of vodka and the evening ended with Dylan and Aly promising to return. As soon as they were alone in the helicopter cabin, Dylan said, "That was an all-around nice day."

Aly met his gaze then looked away. "It really was."

After a brief lull, Dylan felt he needed to say something. "I'm back on set tomorrow. The plan is for everyone to go. Don't feel that you have to stay if it gets boring. Sometimes it takes a while to get it right and that means a lot of repetition."

Her eyes met his again. "I'm looking forward to seeing the process."

"Oh, it's a process. I'm still learning how to make a fight

scene look authentic without it being real."

"Uh oh."

The memory still pained him. "I've trained for how to do it, but in the heat of the moment I forgot. I had to hit the ground, roll onto my feet, and sock him in the face. I broke his nose."

Aly tried and failed to look sympathetic before she gave in to the humor of it and smiled. "I'm sorry, I know that's horrible, but I'm imagining how that went over."

"Not well, let me tell you. Actors are all about the perfection of their features. This particular actor played a boxer in his last movie so he came in with a huge ego. So smug, the type who likes to intimidate people, especially if they're in a position where they can't speak up."

"Sounds like breaking his nose might not have been an accident."

"I'd like to think I'm above that." The memory brought a smile to his face. "But it did feel good. He got all teary like it was the first time in his life anyone had ever hit him. I offered him the opportunity to hit me back, but he left in an ambulance. An ambulance for a broken nose? It was ridiculous and the opposite of who he tries to convince people he is."

"I wasn't there to see his injury so I can't say for sure, but my guess is I would have diagnosed him with a severe case of you-got-what-you-deserve."

Dylan laughed. "Love it. Yes. Anyway, that's one of the scenes we couldn't redo earlier because his nose was swollen. I intend to be on my best behavior, though, because the quicker I get these scenes finished the more time I can spend with—" He'd almost said *you*, but stopped himself and instead said, "—everyone."

"Will you be working all week?"

He shrugged. "I'm hoping for just a few days. Not sure how long everyone will stay now that we're not moving onto the island, but it would be nice to have some time to hang out."

Before they said more, the helicopter landed and the pilot was opening the door. Beneath the hum of the blades, Dylan and Aly thanked him then sprinted away toward the lodge.

They stopped at the stairs of the deck. Aly looked up at him. He'd never wanted to kiss someone more. "Thank you, Dylan. It really was a perfect day."

He wasn't the type to hesitate or second-guess, but they'd made an agreement of sorts. He could almost hear the Icelandic woman reminding him to be patient. If he stayed the course, he was in a win/win situation. Worst case? They remained good friends, and who didn't need more of those? Best case?

His cock instantly hardened and he groaned. *Okay, so less imagining the best case unless I want everyone to know how she makes me feel.*

He cleared his throat. "Iceland is an incredible country. I'd love to show you more of it."

"I'd really like that."

He told himself it was his imagination, but the air between them seemed to pulse with sexual energy. *She either has the hots for me, or my cock should send some of my blood back up to my brain so I'll stop seeing what isn't there.*

A car pulled into the driveway. A smiling Connor poured out of one side of the back of it. Angelina appeared out of the other side, looking windblown but happy as well. Connor waved then posed with his legs braced apart, hand on one hip, sword in the air. His legs were covered to the knee in fur boots that matched his outfit: black leggings, a tunic with silver accents, and a flowing fur cape. Angelina went to stand beside him, striking a pose of her own. She was decked out in a bright red, ankle-length gown with fur trim. They looked like caricatures of Vikings, but they were embracing it.

"Oh, boy," Dylan said.

"Be healthy and happy," Connor boomed.

Angelina puffed up her chest, deepened her voice and said, "When ships were made of wood, men were made of steel." Then she smiled and swayed. "Women too."

And a little drunk. The two exchanged a look then burst out laughing like children sharing a joke.

Smiling, Aly glanced up at Dylan. "They're wasted."

"You think?" he answered with a chuckle. "That must have been some adventure."

Connor waved his sword high in the air. "Where wolf teeth are ears. No. That's not it." He shook his head, tossed his sword to the side and said, "Come woman, the time for talking is done." With that he swung Angelina up and over his shoulder then stumbled back several feet, looking as if he might land on his ass.

Dylan rushed forward, grabbed him by the arm and righted him. "Easy there, Connor. This doesn't seem like a good idea."

"Are you doubting that a Viking can carry his woman off to his bed?"

Aly went to his other side and tilted her head toward Angelina's. "You might want to tell your man to put you down before the two of you get hurt."

Slurring her words slightly, Angelina pouted then slapped Connor in the ass. "Don't you dare drop me and kill my Viking fantasy."

"Grab an arm," Dylan said across Connor.

Aly did and the two made sure Connor made it up the steps and into the house. Once inside, with Angelina still slung over his shoulder, Connor said, "Good night friends. I've got it from here." He turned on his heel and strode away with a waving, smiling Angelina.

Aly covered her mouth with one hand. "I doubt either of them will be feeling good in the morning."

"But what a memory," Dylan said.

She glanced up at him then away. "I wouldn't have thought they would get on as well as they do, but you can tell they like each other as well as love each other."

He nodded. "That's what matters most, I'd guess. I imagine everything else comes and goes." As he said the words he realized how much he meant them. He didn't just want to fuck Aly, he wanted what both of his siblings had found—a friend, partner, lover. Could Aly be that? He didn't know, but he was willing to put the time into finding out.

Their gaze met and held. She licked her bottom lip. "It's late and you should get to bed early so you're sharp tomorrow."

It was nearly impossible to imagine walking away from her. "I should."

"Aly, you're back," Joanna said as she entered the room. "How was your day?"

Dylan held in a groan of frustration and told himself the interruption was for the best. Nothing he wanted to do with Aly involved rushing. "I have to be on the set early so I'll let you two ladies chat. Good night, Joanna. Aly."

"Good night," Aly said in a slightly breathless tone.

He made his way to the bathroom they shared and took his second cold shower of the day.

Chapter Nine

THE NEXT MORNING on a closed-off street in a tiny town that sat on the edge of a fjord, Dylan went over the mechanics of the fight scene they were reshooting that day. The lack of warmth he'd received when greeting the man playing his opponent was disappointing, but not unexpected. Dylan had heard he'd auditioned for the lead and his ego was still dented from being offered a much smaller role—only one scene in the whole movie.

In the background, Dylan heard the director calling out instructions. Dylan needed to slide across the hood of a car at a speed that implied he was out of control, fall, tuck and roll, and come to a stop right in front of the other actor—where he was instructed to rise to his feet and deliver a pulled punch that would lead into the choreographed fight scene.

Somewhere in the back of his head he was aware that his friends and family were watching, but years of playing football had taught him how to block out the noise. He refused to allow himself to look around to see if Aly was there. Just like game day, nothing belonged in his head but his immediate goal. Everything else could wait until the director called, "Cut."

Dylan practiced punching at but not connecting with the side of the car. This time there would be no mistakes. He'd come early to the set and worked with his fight trainer on timing and sequencing. *I've got this.*

On the director's cue, he walked away from the car and started toward it in a flat-out run. Up and over, tuck and roll, he planted his feet and rose to his full height. Before he had a chance to complete the next step, the other actor punched him square in the jaw.

Now some men, men who hadn't spent their lives in bar fights and punching matches with his mountain of a brother, might have been thrown off by the sneak attack. Dylan burst out laughing. *I mean, hell, I deserved it.*

The director called cut and a member of the crew ran over to speak to the other actor. When the man seemed calm enough, Dylan walked over and offered his hand. "Hey, I totally get it. I'm still sorry about your nose. We're even now. Truce?"

"You think this is a joke?" the other man snarled.

Dylan raised both of his hands in surrender. "I shouldn't have laughed. I'm sorry. You took me by surprise."

With a sprinkle of profanity, the other actor went on and on about how the movie would fail because they hired a pretty boy instead of a real actor. He might have also gone on about Dylan having the fight scene skills of a toddler. Possibly. Dylan stopped listening midway and stood there, waiting for him to calm. Actors were notoriously high-strung and Dylan had given up trying to reason with them. Sometimes it was better to just let them vent.

When the man had finally spent his fury, Dylan asked, "So we're good now?"

Bad choice. The man launched himself at Dylan, leading with a hit to the ribs that felt like a child had delivered it. For a few minutes there was a flurry of wild punches that were more annoying than painful. When he stopped, Dylan was smiling. "Seriously, we don't have to do this."

Wrong choice again. In the background, the director yelled for someone to break them up. Someone touched the other man's arm, asking him to calm down and step away. It was one of the female crew members which should have been enough to diffuse the situation, but the actor shoved her away and continued to tell Dylan how untalented he was.

The crew member started to fall backward. Dylan reached out to steady her and was taken by surprise by a strong kick to the stomach from the actor. Dylan was already off-balance and this sent him down to his knees just shy of where the crew member hit the dirt.

Dylan rose to his feet, helped the woman up and very slowly turned toward the actor who suddenly didn't look as brave. "Get your shit and get off this set. I don't care what it takes, but you're not in this movie. And if I see you touch anyone else, it'll be more than your nose that gets broken."

When the man looked about to say something else, Dylan stepped forward, towering over him, and the man backed away. The director was there after that, yelling for someone to remove the other actor from the area and call the lawyers because he was out.

The woman who'd hit the dirt came to stand next to Dylan. "Thank you."

"See what I get when I hold back a punch?"

She laughed, thanked him again, then stepped aside as the director came over.

"Well that's great," he growled. "Not that I blame you. He won't work again on anything I do, but we need a replacement." He scanned the crowd and stopped dead. "Who's that?"

Dylan followed his gaze. "That's my friend Bradford."

"He's perfect. Get him over here."

"Oh, I don't think he would—" Dylan stopped. "Hold on, I'll see if he's interested."

On his way to do just that he spotted Aly standing off to the side. Sure the director was watching and already upset, but that was often the case. He detoured over to Aly. "Hey."

Her eyebrows rose. "Wow, tell me it's not always like this."

Dylan shrugged. "I felt bad for the guy until he went too far. People like that often do. In this business it's easy to start feeling like you're special, but everyone here is. When you forget that, it's time to find another career."

She smiled. "You're a good guy, Dylan."

"That's why I'm the hero." He was just joking, but to make sure she realized that he winked. Really there wasn't much that felt better than making her smile. "Can't stay and chat, I'm on a mission. Wish me luck."

"Good luck."

With that he walked away and toward where Bradford

was standing beside Joanna. "Hey, Bradford."

"No."

"Hear me out. It's one scene."

"No."

"They don't even need to put your name in the credits."

"No."

"My fight choreographer/trainer is here. He can walk you through the scene with me. If we do it well we could be done in thirty minutes."

"Not interested."

It was what he expected. Dylan normally would have given up there. Instead he decided to take a page out of Connor's book. "I'll let you really punch me."

"No." A small smile lifted the corners of Bradford's mouth. "You'd feel mine."

Trying to look disinterested in the outcome, Dylan lifted and lowered a shoulder. "Hey, if you're too afraid to do it, I get it. Fight scenes are more difficult than actual fights. You have to think and remain in control." He sighed. "A shame, though, because I bet the producer would have donated your salary to Joanna's horse rescue."

Sure, it was low, but when Joanna hugged Bradford's side and exclaimed, "Oh, Bradford, please. You'd be amazing on the big screen."

He growled deep in his chest and said, "One scene. And we do it in one take."

"Okay, then let's walk you through it." Dylan waved for his fight trainer to join them. As he turned he caught Aly's gaze and mouthed, "He said yes."

She made a big thumbs-up.

A short time later, after several practice fights, just before the director called for everyone to take their places, Dylan gave Bradford a light punch to the shoulder. "Now that you know how to do this without hurting me, remember that's an option."

Bradford's mouth twitched. "Where would the fun be in that?"

Dylan laughed. Bradford didn't join in. Dylan told himself he was most likely joking. He was seventy-five percent sure he was anyway.

After walking a good distance from the car, Dylan took off in a run toward it. He was on it sliding, rolling, then back to his feet on the other side where Bradford was standing. Dylan sent a powerful punch toward his head, but pulled back before connecting.

Just as they'd practiced, Bradford came back with a hit that sent Dylan backward . . . pain free. After that, the two flew through the moves they'd practiced with precision and when he delivered the fake knockout punch, Bradford crumpled to the ground.

"Cut," the director called. "That's a wrap. Meet on the dock tomorrow morning for the yacht scene." With that the crew began to pack up.

Dylan leaned forward and offered Bradford a hand. Bradford took it and Dylan hauled him easily to his feet. "You were awesome," Dylan said.

Joanna rushed in, beaming. "That was incredible. You're a star, Bradford."

"Hardly." He hugged Joanna, then looked at Dylan and said, "I didn't expect to enjoy that at all, but it was really interesting, thanks."

"You're welcome." Dylan looked around. Aly had a huge grin on her face and shot him a double thumbs-up and his heart soared.

LUSTING AFTER A man who was in the friend category was confusing enough, but constantly finding new reasons to like him was downright frustrating. Aly wanted to shake Dylan and demand that he do something juvenile before she did something worse like fall for him.

That morning she'd assured herself that being on set would bring out a different side of him. It hadn't. Everything she already knew about him had also come across during his altercation with the other actor.

Dylan was above average height, built, and if stories were to be believed had been in more than his fair share of brawls. It wasn't shocking that a punch from an actor who had probably lived a much softer life had left Dylan unfazed.

That Dylan had found humor in the situation also hadn't been out of norm for him. Nor was the fact that he'd maintained a certain amount of sympathy for the other actor until he pushed a member of the crew.

Watching Dylan stand up for the woman and back the other actor down was panty-wetting sexy. God, no man had the right to be that sexy. A glance around confirmed that Aly wasn't the only one who felt that way. Half the crew, both men and women, were looking at him in adoration the same way she was.

When he'd gone over to talk to Bradford, Aly had been silently cheering him on. So many in Dylan's situation would have become arrogant and demanding, but it had been his humility and humor that had won Bradford over. Participating in that one scene had also given Bradford something else to think about beside how the trip had started and that was a gift in itself.

I need to spend less time with Dylan because the more time we're together the more I wonder why we can't be more than friends.

Oh, yes, outside of the small hurdle of him not being interested in me.

The man can swim naked with me without getting excited. Really, no further evidence is required to convince me that he doesn't feel the same way I do.

Still smiling from his talk with Bradford, Dylan walked over to where Aly was standing. "The next scene requires substantial setup so we'll be shooting it tomorrow. That means we have the rest of the day off. Joanna suggested we head to Reykjavik, walk around and have an early meal. They aren't feeling so well."

Shocking. "Sounds perfect. You probably have to make it an early night again tonight."

He nodded. "Tomorrow will be a longer day. The good news is we might be able to get all the scenes finished and then I'm free."

After a pause, she said, "Today was really interesting. And you're very talented."

He gave her a long look. "Thanks. There's still so much I don't know, but that keeps the whole experience fresh."

Another lull in their conversation. She was curious about something and finally just blurted, "When I saw the other actor shove a member of the crew, I thought for sure you were going to break his nose again."

"A year ago I would have." He ran a hand through his hair. "I might not have asked for any of this, but I'm grateful for it. The Barringtons have not only been good to my sister, but to my whole family. Clay might be over-the-top, but he vouched for Connor and me and that was what made this career possible for us. Claire did a good job of explaining how an ounce of restraint is more valuable than an ocean of apology."

"Wow, that's powerful."

"Besides, that little shit wanted me to punch him back. He decided he was a victim and I was the bad guy. You can't talk people out of that mindset once they choose it."

Too true. "When he hit you and you laughed—you're lucky he didn't have a weapon."

Dylan shrugged. "I don't understand how someone who starred in a boxing movie can't punch. Hell, I hit Viviana harder than that when we were kids."

Her eyes rounded. "You hit your sister?"

"Oh, don't worry, Viviana looks all sweet and cultured now, but she's a Tasmanian devil. Never arm wrestle her, I've seen her bring grown men to tears. My father raised me to never hit a girl, but when we were young Viviana would come charging in and I had to defend myself."

"I can't picture your sister like that."

"We were little. Viviana evolved before the rest of us, but don't let her fool you—at her core she'll always be a Sutton."

Aly smiled. "I'll remember that."

He searched her face. "Every woman should know how to defend herself. Have you ever taken a self-defense course?"

"Can't say that I have."

"What would you do if someone attacked you?"

"Scream?"

He frowned. "I'm serious. You should learn some basic techniques. With the right moves you could even take down someone like me."

"I appreciate your concern, but I'm fine."

"I could teach you."

Her heart started to race. "Teach me?"

"Some defensive moves. In my hometown they had a free community course and often asked me to be the mock aggressor. You know, because I'm—"

"Thank you—no." Just imagining how good wrestling with him would feel was torture enough.

He shrugged. "The offer is there if you decide you want to try it. I consider it something everyone should know, not just women."

"If I change my mind, I'll tell you."

Angelina called to them, asking if they were ready to head out. Dylan reached out and touched her arm lightly. "Aly . . ."

Warmth spread through her. She fought to conceal her reaction to his touch. "We should go."

He dropped his hand. The world around them disappeared and for just a moment she could have sworn he was fighting back the desire to kiss her. Lord knew she was close to throwing herself into his arms.

Then he shook his head and began walking toward the rest of the group. She fell into step beside him, kicking herself for not giving him the chance to say whatever it was he was holding back.

Chapter Ten

A FEW DAYS later Dylan was in his room repacking his luggage when there was a knock on his door. "One minute." His breath caught in his throat and he stashed his underwear beneath his jeans. Although after filming had wrapped up he and Aly had spent time together, it had always been with the group. No random meetups by the hot tub. No talks on the side. He was beginning to think he'd done something to offend her and that she was avoiding him.

Maybe, though, like him, she didn't want the trip to come to an end without making plans to see each other again. He opened the door and let out a sigh. "Clay."

As if unaware of the lack of enthusiasm in Dylan's greeting, Clay entered. "We're heading home tomorrow," he said even though they'd all agreed to earlier.

Dylan referenced the luggage on his bed. "I'll be ready."

Clay walked to the center of the room then thumbed toward the door. "Anything going on between you and you know? This is a pretty convenient setup if there is."

"Not a thing."

Clay nodded and pocketed his hands. "That's a shame. For a while there I thought you had something—then it just fizzled out. Disappointing."

Rolling his shoulders back, Dylan said, "It didn't 'fizzle out.'"

"Because there was never anything there."

"Clay, I know what you're doing and it's not going to work. Aly and I are friends. That's it."

One of Clay's eyebrows arched. "But is that how you want it to be?"

Dylan shrugged. "It's what she wants."

"Is it?"

Dylan rubbed a hand over his forehead. "Clay, I count you as one of my best friends."

Clay's face lit up at that.

Dylan continued, "But that doesn't mean you're not sometimes annoying as all hell."

That narrowed Clay's eyes. "Pardon me for showing interest in a situation you are clearly fumbling."

"There is no situation, Clay."

"Bok bok bok."

Dylan's mouth dropped open. "Are you seriously making chicken noises at me?"

"Bok bok bokity bok bok."

Shaking his head, Dylan laughed. "You have spent way too much time with Connor lately."

"Bok."

"It has nothing to do with me being afraid."

"Bok?"

And this was the side of Clay that made it impossible for one to take Clay seriously or be upset with him. On one hand the world was one big joke to him; on the other hand no one would fight harder for you. It was an unusual combination—but that was Clay. "Fine, I find her attractive. If she weren't part of our social circle, I might have already come on stronger. But—and this is a big but—she's practically family now. There won't be many events in Connor's life she won't be part of. I'm trying to be responsible here and see the bigger picture. If something happens between us, it happens. If it doesn't, I want her to be comfortable around me."

Clay groaned. "You are so much less fun since you grew up."

"Thanks?"

"Where are you headed after this?"

"I thought I'd go visit my father first, then I'm not sure."

"Don't go too far. I'm not announcing it yet, but I'm planning something big for Joanna and Bradford and attendance is mandatory. Joanna doesn't know, so don't say anything."

Mandatory. It wasn't worth trying to explain to Clay that some people sent invitations and allowed people the option of refusing. "How soon?"

"A couple of weeks."

"I'll make sure I'm around."

Clay nodded toward Aly's room. "I'm two for two, you know. After all I've done for you, you might want to consider giving me a chance."

"Not happening, Clay."

"That's what everyone says. Why do you all make it so difficult?"

"You do realize you're not actually a Fairy Godfather, right?"

That didn't win Dylan any points. Clay's eyes narrowed again. "I'm giving you two weeks to figure this out on your own, then I'll show you who is and who isn't *extraordinaire*."

Dylan laughed. Really, at this point, would it matter? She felt the way she felt. "Deal."

A smile returned to Clay's face. "I knew you'd come around. How exciting. I can't wait to tell Lexi—she denies it, but she enjoys this as much as I do."

"I'm sure she does."

Clay's expression turned more serious. "I'm glad we came to watch you film. You're always crediting me for your success, but all I did was open the door. You walked through it and made the room yours. I'm proud of you."

Not too much brought Dylan to the edge of tears, but his eyes misted up. "Get the fuck out of here, Clay. Don't you have trouble to cause anywhere else?"

Clay nodded. "See you at breakfast." And he walked out of the room.

Alone again, Dylan sat on the edge of his bed and slammed his hand into the side of his luggage.

I'm not fumbling anything.

Aly said she wanted to be friends. I'm honoring that.

It's the fucking right thing to do.

He stood and paced to the other side of his room and

back, glaring at the door that connected to the bathroom he and Aly shared. *What else am I supposed to do? Knock on that door? Lean in? Kiss her?*

Yep, that's all it took for him to become painfully aroused. *If it were my sister in there I'd want the man in the next room to keep his dick in his pants and be respectful.*

And that's exactly what I'm doing.

He sighed.

I'm right here, Aly. It's our last night. You want me—you know where to find me.

IN HER OWN room, Aly paused while packing. She heard voices in Dylan's room and was tempted to step into the bathroom so she could hear, but the sting from what she'd overheard the first time she'd eavesdropped was still too fresh. *Yeah, that's not how I want this vacation to end.* The week had already had enough highs and lows to give a person whiplash.

Once Aly had realized how close she was to having serious feelings for Dylan she knew she needed to put a little distance between them. Despite spending the rest of the week using the group as a buffer, Aly felt proud of how far she'd pushed herself beyond her comfort zone. If it weren't for a lingering excessive amount of sexual attraction to him, they might have become great friends.

We went skinny-dipping. No one can't say I can't lower my guard with a man.

She resumed packing, folding each item carefully into efficient tight bundles. As she did she relived the best of the week. Together, she and the group watched Dylan finish filming, toured glaciers, rode Icelandic horses, and even learned to cook a traditional lamb dish.

Everywhere they went people recognized Dylan and Connor. It was interesting to watch both handle their newfound fame. Connor bounded up with a big warm smile and a hug if someone asked for it. He posed happily, introduced Angelina as the love of his life and left his fans laughing.

Dylan drew just as much of a crowd, but they came to him rather than the other way around. His smile was more guarded at first, but welcoming. He asked more questions than Connor. He liked to know their names and where they were from. If they had children he hunkered down to introduce himself and spoke to them in a way that had them chattering back about themselves, completely forgetting that he was the famous one.

Before she'd taken the time to get to know him, she'd assumed Dylan was vain and that all the attention he received had gone to his head. He wasn't and it hadn't. She had yet to find something she didn't like about him though she'd tried to.

Which was one reason she was glad the vacation was coming to an end. Everyone had faults. Dylan surely had them. It was concerning that she couldn't see them.

More concerning was how hard it was to imagine that as of tomorrow he would once again not be part of her life. Yes, they'd see each other at events, but that would be it. Her stomach churned at the idea of returning to that.

She told herself what she was feeling was a false sense of attachment triggered by a shared horrific event. *Like disaster survivors.*

It'll pass when I'm home and back in my regular life.

When she'd finished packing all but what she would need that night and the next morning, she grabbed a towel and headed for the shower. She'd already started the water, stepped out of her clothing, placed them in a neat pile, and was about to step into the shower when she realized she hadn't locked the door on his side.

That would only be a problem if I thought he would come in—and even that would only be a problem if I'd mind.

She shook her head, laughed at herself, and stepped beneath the hot spray of water. As she soaped her body, she closed her eyes and imagined hearing the door open. He'd strip just outside the shower and step in without even asking. Her heart was racing and she moaned as she imagined him behind her, running his hands along her back and the curve of her ass. Her nipples hardened beneath her hands as they became his hands in her mind.

When she turned, the hot water became his hungry mouth. She parted her mouth and her legs. Her hand, his hand, wandered down to her sex. So strong. So sure. She leaned against the cool tiles of the shower and gave herself over to the pleasure of his imagined caress.

She was warming.

Rising.

Getting deliciously close to release.

"Aly?" a voice called into the bathroom.

Aly straightened in a rush, dropping her hand from herself and she slipped, screaming as she fell to the floor of the shower in a splat. *Owwwww.*

"Do you have a hair tie I can borrow? I'm already packed and can't find mine." *Joanna.* "Are you in the shower? I can come back."

"Please do," Aly said as she pushed herself up to her feet. Her ass as well as one of her shoulders was smarting. "How about I bring it to you?"

"Awesome, thanks!"

"Aly?" This time it was Dylan. "I thought I heard a scream. Are you okay?"

"I'm fine." Stepping out of the shower, Aly wiped some of the steam from the mirror and checked her backside. Yep, two big red spots where she'd connected. *Well, that's what I get for masturbating in someone else's house.* A thought occurred to her and she smiled. *Everyone in heaven has a death story. Imagine telling that one for eternity.*

Masturbation was natural and even healthy, but no one wanted to die doing it.

She wrapped a towel around herself, then another around her hair.

"I thought you'd fallen," Dylan called out.

"I did, but I bounce well."

"Did you hit your head? If so you should have someone stay with you."

In my fantasy he would offer himself.

But Dylan added, "Want me to get Angelina or Joanna?"

See, that's why I'm the problem. He's just a good guy who

simply isn't into me. Not a crime. I should be grateful that my friends have surrounded themselves with such considerate people. "I landed on my ass—no risk of concussion, but thank you."

She thought that was the end of it, but as she prepared to walk out of the bathroom and back into her bedroom, he asked, "Aly, we're good, right? I just want to make sure I didn't say or do anything that upset you. I've really enjoyed getting to know you this week."

She stopped and glanced back at his door. It was all that separated them. What would he do if she opened it and dropped her towel? Her body was still revved from her own touch, it would explode from his.

She thought back over the week. He'd been nothing but a gentleman. Kind. Attentive. A good friend.

That's what sex would be between us—a friend fuck.

Usually I can handle that, but this is different.

I don't know why, it just is.

"We're good, Dylan. I enjoyed getting to know you too. This has been a week I'll always remember."

"Me too."

When he didn't say anything she returned to her room, closed the door behind her and took a deep breath. *This isn't how I'll feel next week.*

As soon as I'm back in my own life all of this will fade away.

Chapter Eleven

A FEW DAYS later Dylan was sitting on the back porch of his father's house throwing a ball for Button. The amount of slobber the game involved was only forgivable because of the joy it brought the young Saint Bernard.

His father came out to join him, a bottle of beer in each hand. He tossed one to Dylan who caught it easily and flipped off the cap on the same corner of the steps he had through the years he hadn't been old enough to drink but had anyway. A little beer never harmed anyone, not in his opinion.

"It was great to have both of my boys home."

Dylan nodded and took a swig of his beer. "Good to be home."

"I was surprised when you didn't head back to the city with Connor and Angelina."

"I need a little more time to decompress."

"Take as long as you need. This will always be your home." His father sat beside him on the top step of the porch. "That was some vacation you all had in Iceland. I'm glad no one was hurt."

Dylan drank down a good portion of his beer. "Our lives sure have changed, haven't they? Remember when our biggest concern was who Connor would have sex with next?"

His father chuckled and referenced the gray in his hair. "All three of you gave me these. Do you remember the year I built a garage for your principal? You were what—twelve? It was a bribe to keep all of your asses from getting suspended. I know you never went looking for fights, but you could have walked away from a few more than you did. Viviana too."

With a mock gasp, Dylan said, "My father is corrupt? I always thought you were the good one among us."

He smiled. "Where do you think you get your *trouble* gene?"

Dylan placed his bottle on the step beside him. "Mom would agree. She used to tell me stories about you." One story came back to him that matched what he hadn't yet been able to shake from his thoughts. "She told me you were positive you were meant for each other from the moment you met—even though she was dating someone else at the time."

His father shrugged. "Dating is for people who are still figuring things out. I never looked at a married woman in my life and I never would. Besides, she took my number. A woman doesn't do that if she's in love."

Dylan picked up his beer and finished it. "What does it mean if you don't know? Does it mean it's not meant to be?"

"Oh, hold on, you met someone."

"More like I know someone. You know her too, but I'm

not sure I want to start tossing her name around."

"Connor told me you were sweet on Angelina's friend Aly. The doctor. I approve."

Fucking Connor. "Seems like holding back her name is no longer necessary."

"Connor has always told me everything. He charges forward without worrying too much about what could go wrong. Thankfully he loves the same way." His father gave Dylan a pat on the back. "Now you, you were always more like your mother. She thought about things a good long time before she made her move, but when she did she poured her heart and soul into the course she chose." He took a drink. "I was damned lucky she chose me, but it took her a bit to choose."

Dylan's heart warmed at the idea that some of the good of his mother lived on in him. "Aly said she wants to be friends. I've respected that, but now I'm wondering if I should have tested the waters a little more. I didn't want her to feel uncomfortable, but by playing it so cool I might have slotted myself permanently into the friend zone."

His father gave him a long look. "I'm proud of you, son. So many people care more about what they want than what others do. There's a reason you're so well-liked in this town and it has nothing to do with your fame."

"One good fight makes a good friend?"

With another chuckle, his father said, "No, although you probably have scrapped with half the men in town. No, they like you because they understand where your heart has always been. Your family, your friends, your team, this town.

When you, Connor, and Viviana took over the charity your mother started and continued pouring money into it even when you didn't have much to give—they knew. When their siblings went to a party you were at, whether they were boys or girls, you made sure no one bothered them. There's a lot of people here who would go to battle for you if you ever needed them."

Dylan's cheeks warmed. He wasn't used to his father laying on praise quite so thick. "Are you buttering me up for something, Dad?"

"Not at all. I just want you to see that your way has never been the wrong way." He picked up the drool-covered ball and threw it for Button. "I'm also glad you struck out on your own. You and Connor have always been close, but you needed room to figure out who you are away from him."

Not much got by their father. "I did and I have."

"Good."

They sat in comfortable silence for a long time with Button retrieving the ball and giving it to one of them to throw again. There was a comfort to the rhythm of home that Dylan found nowhere else. One day he hoped he could say the same about a place of his own. "You never chased Mom. You just waited for her, knowing she would come to you."

"Well, I did tell her to call me if she was looking for a good man who could imagine forever with her."

"You've got some big balls there, Dad."

His father looked pensive. "Only when it came to her. I can see why you'd tread more carefully with Aly, though. If she's interested in you, Dylan, don't worry, she'll give you a sign."

Dylan threw the ball far enough that Button was out of breath and done with the game when he returned. "She did go skinny-dipping with me." His father's eyes rounded. "It's not uncommon in Iceland. And we weren't alone. Okay, we were at first but nothing happened. And then the farmer's family showed up." That didn't sound better. "Seriously, Dad, it was nothing."

His father scratched his cheek and made a face, but didn't say anything. It was far from being the first time they'd accidentally entered into a conversation they decided to backpedal out of. In fact, Dylan distinctly remembered when he officially became a teenager and his father had wanted to make sure he would practice safe sex. He came in, talked around the subject of sex in a confusing manner, then tossed a box of condoms and a pamphlet at him and fled.

When the time had come to tell Connor, Dylan had had the talk with him and Connor had raided his stash of condoms ever since. Really, looking back, he should have made sex sound more dangerous.

Viviana? She'd been on her own as far as that subject.

"You went swimming in the nude with her?" his father asked in a tone that was deceptively calm.

Dylan cleared his throat. "I did."

"And you're still waiting for a sign that she might be into you?" His father threw back his head and laughed. "No wonder Connor always got laid more than you."

"Dad!"

His father tried to cough back another laugh, then waved

his hand as it burst out anyway. Dylan had no choice but to wait him out. When he finally regained control of himself, he said, "I'm sorry, you're right, you keep right on waiting and who knows someday she might give you a hint about how she feels." After a moment, his father put his arm around Dylan. "Does Connor know?"

"I didn't tell him."

"Can I?" With that his father started laughing again while giving Dylan a shake as a message to lighten up.

A smile pulled at Dylan's mouth. "You're both dicks, you know that." He started to laugh along. "I love you, but sometimes I have no idea why."

His father stood. "You get that from your mother as well. Come on, with the extra money you've been sending back, made it possible to finally break ground where the Sutton Technical School will be. People are getting excited to soon have an option for students who don't want the four-year route but want to learn a trade. People are already sending applications from all over, even though we're not accepting any yet. It was a good idea. Let's go see how it's coming along."

Dylan rose to his feet as well. "Sometimes I have good ideas."

"You do. When do you think you'll see Aly again?"

"We'll both be at Joanna's rescue when Bradford proposes. About a week and a half."

"Normally I'd suggest calling her earlier, but my guess is you have that woman all turned around and confused. Give her a little time to miss you. It'll go better."

"Don't say anything to Connor." He wagged a finger at his father.

"I won't, but if holding it in gives me a stroke that's on you."

It was Dylan's turn to laugh. Button nudged at his hand with a disgustingly slimy ball. "You'll survive, but if you don't, make sure you leave Button to Connor in your will."

A WEEK LATER, in her office in a hospital in New Jersey, Aly stood and stretched. Since the Iceland trip, she'd packed her schedule. She'd told herself it was because she needed to catch up, but the truth was she'd wanted to wipe Dylan out of her head.

He was proving to be a more stubborn issue than she'd anticipated. Memories of him met her at the door of her empty apartment and lingered in her thoughts through the night. She kept herself firmly planted in the moment when she was with a patient, but reading emails was proving difficult. She was used to being able to speed read and retain information with a clarity that was above average. Since Iceland she found herself pausing halfway through an email and having to return to the beginning to reread it.

On the street she thought she saw Dylan a few times, but it was never him. She gave in twice and watched *Doubled Danger*—to torture herself, apparently, because it left her feeling worse rather than better.

Countless times she took out her phone and almost called him. There was no reason she couldn't—they were friends. Which was also the same reason she didn't call him.

She was angry with herself for hoping he would call her. They'd both been clear. This was what they'd agreed to.

I'm losing my mind. I'm going to see him in a few days. I need to get control of this.

A visiting doctor had asked her out. He was handsome and brilliant. She hadn't been the slightest bit tempted.

She walked from her desk to the window behind it, looking out over the visitor parking lot with cars coming and going. She wondered who they were coming to see and hoped whoever it was went home with them.

Because being alone is hard.

She fisted her hand at her side. *What is wrong with me? I have an amazing life. My career is everything I hoped it would be. I love my friends. I don't need some big, dumb movie star to complete me.*

She sighed. *Except, he's not dumb.*

And I feel his absence. I didn't know that was possible.

The buzz of her phone was a welcome distraction. Angelina started talking without wasting time on niceties. "I'm so excited about this weekend I'm dying."

Aly chuckled. "I'm excited too, but I'm confident neither of us is dying."

"I can't even talk to Joanna this week. I'm too afraid I'll spill the beans."

"I've been avoiding her too." *Because of that as well as a lack of desire to answer questions about Dylan.*

"Have you heard from Dylan?" Angelina asked.

And here we go. "No, nor did I expect to."

"Oh, that's a shame. Well, you'll see him at Joanna's."

Built-up frustration spilled out. "Could we not talk about Dylan?"

"Sure. Did something happen?"

"No. I don't want to do this right now. I'm tired and—"

"I'm sorry."

Aly instantly felt bad for snapping. "No, I am. I'm doing everything I can to stop thinking about him."

"And failing?"

"Completely."

"Oh, Aly. This is good."

"It doesn't feel good. I can't eat. I can't sleep. I'm getting less intelligent by the day."

Angelina made a sympathetic sound. "Have you considered calling him?"

"I have. Fundamentally I have no issue with women calling men. I've asked men out before. I don't get it. I take out my phone and just sit there staring at it."

"You're scared."

There was no need to lie to someone who would see through it anyway. "I am. What is wrong with me?"

"Absolutely nothing. You lowered your guard and that's scary. Asking out a man who doesn't matter is easy. It's totally different when he's someone you can't get out of your head."

She did understand. "Yes."

"Want my advice?"

"Always."

"You're going to see him in a few days anyway, so you might as well wait. Seeing Bradford propose to Joanna is going to be an emotional experience for all of us. Leave your heart open to possibilities."

"Listen to you. This wasn't how you sounded before Connor."

"Exactly. I used to hold on tightly to my emotions because I was afraid if I opened up to someone I'd get hurt again. What I realized was that I hurt a lot more when I was all closed up. Relationships aren't for the fainthearted, but I wouldn't want to go back—no matter what happens. I would rather love and lose than ever be afraid like that again."

Aly nodded. "I would never have described myself as a fearful person, but I guess we all have our vulnerabilities. I don't know what I feel for Dylan, but it's definitely different than how I've felt about anyone before him. I want more than friendship."

"Then when you see him this weekend you should tell him. Who knows, he might feel the same way."

Aly let out a shaky breath. "Right. Just tell him."

Oh, God.

Chapter Twelve

DRIVING TO JOANNA'S rescue with Connor, Angelina, and her son Whitney turned out to be just the distraction Dylan needed. They talked about soccer camp, movies, and what Iceland had been like. Dylan was relieved that Whitney didn't appear to know anything about the way that trip had begun. Connor could keep a secret when it mattered.

They drove up Joanna's long driveway and parked next to another car. The couple who greeted them were Joanna's parents and they were every bit as warm and friendly as Dylan had guessed they would be. Huggy people, but Dylan didn't mind. Farther up the driveway Joanna and Bradford were each in different horse paddocks with the horses they must have been working with before people started to arrive. Joanna was waving toward them, looking confused but happy.

Another car pulled in and parked. Aly. Dylan's hands went sweaty then cold. He rolled his shoulders back and told himself to relax. Seeing her again was sending his body into overload, though. He wanted to pick her up, carry her off to somewhere they could talk without an audience.

Angelina bolted over to meet Aly with a hug. Joanna's parents were next, chattering about how excited they were. "Joanna has no idea," her mother exclaimed.

Her father added, "Poor Bradford looks nervous. I remember that feeling."

Dylan glanced over to where Bradford was letting himself out of the horse paddock. He did look nervous. It was good to see the human side of him.

"Hi," Aly said from right in front of Dylan, taking him by surprise. She was in a form-fitting dress that highlighted all the parts of her he'd already seen and would have found distracting even if she'd had them better covered. Was the cleavage she was showing for his benefit? God, he hoped so.

"Hey." He moved forward to hug her, then hesitated.

She seemed to do the same.

Dylan's vision narrowed until there was only her and how much he'd missed her. He wanted to ask her how she became more beautiful every time he saw her. He fought a desire to pull her to him and kiss her until his feelings for her were clear to not only her but everyone. His blood rushed south as he looked her over again. "Nice"—he almost said dress, ass, *everything* but Whitney was right beside her and Dylan already felt like he was being too obvious about how he felt—"weather today," he finished.

She blinked a few times. "Perfect for a proposal."

He needed to get her alone, even if just for a moment. "Aly—"

"Yes?"

"Dylan!" Sophie, the matriarch of the Barrington clan, called out from behind him. Dylan turned to greet her and was enveloped in a hug. Her husband, Dale, shook Dylan's hand.

"Good to see you, Dylan. We offered to pick up your father, but he's riding over with Viviana and Grant." Another car pulled into the driveway. "That might be them now."

It was, and they were leading a parade of cars full of family and friends. There was a flurry of handshaking and hugging. All of the Barringtons were there but Dylan wasn't surprised. Whether Bradford fully understood it yet or not, they considered him one of them. Sophie and Dale might not have been able to protect their family from tragedy, but they'd weathered those storms and taught their children how to love strong and stand together.

When Sophie moved on to hug Aly, Dylan watched the exchange. Aly accepted the show of affection with awkward acceptance. It made him want to go back and redo how he'd greeted Aly. She needed more hugs in her life.

Viviana and Grant appeared with their son, Sean. He'd seen them a week ago while visiting his father, but still marveled at how quickly his nephew was growing. How was he no longer an infant? Before they knew it, he'd be walking. Grant handed Sean over to Dylan who held him up over his head and made silly faces until little Sean was laughing.

Cuddling Sean to his chest, Dylan smiled at Aly. "Look at this little guy. Doesn't he look just like me?"

Her eyes widened as if she hadn't expected him to address her. She opened her mouth, but said nothing, as if she'd been about to then changed her mind.

"Oh, look," Angelina exclaimed. "It's a Cinderella carriage. Clay, you sure know how to bring it."

Clay adjusted each of his jacket sleeves in turn. "I do."

Lexi clapped her hands together. "This is so romantic. I love being part of it."

A hush fell over the farm. Dressed in a white tux, the carriage driver parked in front of the paddock Joanna was in. One of her staff led away the pony she was working with. Loud enough for all to hear, the driver said, "Joanna Ervin?"

Her response was less audible, but she was nodding.

He continued, "You are hereby invited to spend the rest of your life with a Bradford Wilson. If you're interested in receiving a proposal from him, please step into the carriage."

Dylan glanced at Aly. Her eyes were shining and she was hugging herself. The love she had for her friend was there for everyone to see, no awkwardness, no holding back. He wanted to fill her life with moments like that. It was an intense thought, but it was an emotionally charged setting. Seeing a hardened man like Bradford drop to one knee and profess his love to Joanna made it easy to believe anything was possible.

Dylan sidled closer to Aly and was about to ask her to put aside time for them to talk before the day ended when Sean spit up on his shoulder. "Whoa."

"Oh, my God, sorry, Dylan," Viviana said. "He gets carsick sometimes."

"It's okay," he assured her.

With the ninja skills of a mother, Viviana handed her

son back to her husband and used wipes to clean off Dylan's shoulder. He protested that he was fine then took a few sheets to finish the job. Joanna was on a very short carriage ride to where Bradford was standing and he didn't want to be the reason anyone missed anything.

Once cleaned off, he stepped aside to deposit the sheets in a nearby trash can. When his attention returned to Aly, she was absorbed in the unfolding proposal. She and Angelina were all smiles when Joanna threw her arms around Bradford and he turned to wave to her parents.

All around them, as if by magic, staff appeared with trays of champagne and hors d'oeuvres. Tables covered with white tablecloths and huge bouquets of flowers were set up. The area around Joanna's barn quickly transformed into a luxurious engagement party.

Joanna and Bradford made their way to that area. The couple stopped to thank everyone and dole out hugs. Joanna waved Angelina and Aly over to see her ring.

Connor came to stand beside Dylan. "Your shoulder is wet."

"I know."

"I have an extra shirt in the car." When Dylan gave him a questioning look, he said, "Angelina and I agreed that I won't officially move in until we're married. For now, my trunk is a glorified overnight bag."

It made sense. Although Dylan had cleaned his shirt off, not walking around with a big wet spot on his shoulder that still smelled a little like vomit would be nice. "Thanks. I'll slip away now and be back before anyone even notices."

He left the party area and headed to Connor's car. Once there he rummaged until he found a shirt that looked both clean as well as appropriate for the occasion and pulled his soiled shirt up and over his head.

"Oh, hi, sorry," a female voice that was disappointingly not Aly's said.

"No problem." He tossed his shirt into the trunk before pulling a navy collared oxford over his head. Once he had a moment he recognized her as one of Joanna's barn staff. Someone might have sent her to the cars to retrieve something. "Are you looking for a certain car?"

"Actually, I was hoping to meet you." She got all flushed and starry-eyed. *Crap.* He knew that look. It was how women looked at him when they saw him as "Dylan Sutton the movie star." Still, she worked at a horse rescue, which made her a nice person in his mind. Meeting fans was part of an actor's career. He never understood those who resented them. No, they didn't always appear when it was convenient, but he tried to take a moment to give them an experience that felt personal.

He put out his hand. "Well, hello, then."

She shook his hand, gushing as she did. "I love all your movies."

He released her hand with a chuckle. "I only have one out, but recently finished my second."

Her face went bright red. "I've watched *Doubled Danger* so many times it feels like more than one." She looked even more embarrassed after she spoke.

It was time to get this conversation out from between the

cars and back into the safety of the public eye. He started walking. She fell into step beside him. "Have you worked for Joanna long?"

"I'm a volunteer, but also a freshman in college and considering going into equine medicine."

She's even younger than she looks. That explains a lot. He was tempted to bolt away, but she was someone's little sister and he wouldn't want anyone to be rude to Viviana. "The woman I'm dating is in the medical field as well." It was a white lie, but one that he hoped clarified the situation for her in a painless way. "But she works with humans."

Disappointment flashed in her eyes, then she asked, "Do you think I could take a photo with you? My friends will never believe I met you if I don't."

"Absolutely." He stopped walking and posed with her. "What's your name?"

"Belle Harris." She leaned in and snapped a photo with her phone.

"Beautiful name."

She smiled and took another photo of them. "Thanks."

When she finished he shook her hand again and said, "Well, Belle Harris, it's time for me to return to the party. It was very nice to meet you. I have a feeling you're going to be an amazing horse vet."

She shook his hand vigorously. "Thank you. And thanks for being so nice. I was nervous but I wanted to meet you."

"Best part of my job is all the people I meet through it," he said. In general, he meant it.

They parted as they re-entered the area where the party

was happening. He sought out Aly in the crowd. She met his gaze briefly then looked away. Almost as if she didn't like that he'd been talking to the college student. He decided to ignore the way she turned her back to him and joined her anyway.

It could have been a side effect of watching his friends get engaged, but he was optimistic about how Aly felt toward him. Or it could have been that his father's jokes had woken him up to the possibility that Aly had already given him a very clear sign that she was interested.

Either way, time away from her had helped him decide what he wanted—and he wanted her.

As DYLAN WALKED toward her, Aly told herself she was being ridiculous. They weren't a couple. She was glad she hadn't started the day by blurting out how she felt about him.

She had been in a phenomenal mood. Watching Joanna and Bradford get engaged had been incredibly touching. Unlike the humor of watching Connor and Angelina noodle for catfish and pull out a ring, this proposal had had a fairy-tale quality.

Not that I want anything like that for myself, but Joanna will make a scrapbook about today. And I'll look through it with her a hundred times. It was so beautiful.

Dylan came to stand right beside her. "She's a freshman in college."

"Who?" Her tone held more chill than she'd meant it to.

He gave her a long look. "And here I thought you were

annoyed with me for talking to her."

"Sorry. I have no idea what you're talking about."

He bent to speak near her ear. "You're a horrible liar." As he spoke he put his hand on her lower back; she tensed beneath his touch but only because it sent heat searing through her. "You were jealous."

Aly whipped her head around so she could look up at his face. "I couldn't care less if you flirt with every bubbly blonde in the state."

His laugh was a sexy challenge. "So you did see me with her."

She frowned, opened her mouth, then snapped it shut. She was a highly educated, independent, modern woman. Only he could reduce her to a bumbling, smitten puddle of weakness. Most irritating part, he was likely just having fun with her—expecting her to laugh along—not understanding that there was nothing funny about this for her. "It was hard to miss. She was all over you."

"Hardly." His smile was infuriating. He leaned in again. "Would it help if I said I'd hate watching you talk to some random man?"

That drained the anger right out of her. She searched his face for a hint that he might be joking. "It might, actually."

"I'm in need of medical attention. Since Iceland I've been suffering from a condition called 'I can't get you out of my head.' You're often the first thing I think about in the morning and thoughts of you have been making it damn near impossible to sleep."

She shuddered against him and her body responded faster than her mind. It knew exactly where it wanted this to go. "Whatever this is must be contagious, because I've been exhibiting the same symptoms."

He wrapped his arm around her waist. "I missed you, Aly."

Her heart was beating crazily in her chest. She fought to keep her breathing normal. "I've missed you too."

The way he looked at her, she was sure he was about to kiss her right there in front of everyone. Instead, he just grinned down at her. "I knew you liked me. You had me second-guessing myself for a little bit there, but there were signs."

As she looked up into his beautiful, humor-filled eyes, she felt younger and sexier than she had in a long time. "Like swimming in the nude with you?"

He tipped his head to the side. "See that one got by me. I thought it was all about proving something to yourself."

"It was mostly about that." She would have been lying, though, if she denied how intimate the experience had been. "It was also about allowing myself to be vulnerable with you."

An entirely different expression entered his eyes. "Because you don't normally allow yourself to do that with men."

He understood her so well it was unsettling. "Exactly." She began to tense but fought to keep her walls down. "I've recently realized that I have an unhealthy pattern of choosing men I can't be myself with. They tend to be hyper-critical of me and I tend to be the same with them. Joanna and Angelina suggested that the way to break that pattern was to find someone I could be myself with."

His smile returned. "And you chose me."

"I trust you." As she said the words she realized how much she meant them. Outside of her closest friends, there weren't many people she could say the same about. Dylan was a good man. Strong, but kind. She couldn't imagine him ever intentionally hurting anyone. "I figured even if nothing happened between us I would still have made a step in the right direction."

"You're pretty remarkable, you know that?"

"I suppose." She did and she didn't. She knew her IQ was above average. She considered herself attractive enough to be able to attract sexual partners when she wanted them. Her dedication to her work was noteworthy—but remarkable?

"You are. Some people in your situation would consider themselves a finished product. You have a kick-ass career. You're smarter than most of the people I know, and I know a lot of people. You could sit back and gloat, but you don't. You're still trying to improve and I admire that."

Praise wasn't something she'd received much of in her life and she soaked it in like a flower breaking through snow and discovering the warmth of the sun. "I could say the same about you. You have every reason to be a self-absorbed egomaniac, but somehow you've remained grounded. It says a lot about your character."

"Well, now that we've formed our own mutual appreciation association, what do you think we should do about it?"

The heat in his eyes mirrored the need in hers.

"We could have sex and see how it goes." She expected him to readily agree. Everything about how he was holding her and had been looking at her supported that he wanted to. What confused her was the frown that drew his eyebrows together.

"Would there be a rating system?"

"No." She pulled away from him, and his arm dropped to his side. "Why would you even ask that?"

There it was again, that expression in his eyes she couldn't decipher. "I don't want to have sex like it's part of a clinical trial."

She wanted to understand his reaction, but her defenses were snapping back into place. All she heard was that he didn't want to have sex with her. "No one said you have to. This was a mistake. We're obviously not compatible."

He gently took both of her arms in his hands and turned her toward him. "Look at me."

She didn't for the sole reason that she didn't want to. She kept her gaze fixed on his chest.

"I didn't say I don't want to have sex with you. I said I don't want to do it the way you suggested. I've spent a good deal of the last year fucking people I don't care if I see again. When you and I have sex, I want it to matter."

"Why wouldn't it matter?" She raised her eyes and searched his face. "I don't understand."

He gave her arms a light squeeze. "I know. That's why we need to old school this."

"Old school?"

He nodded. "I'm going to romance you, Aly. Dates. Flowers. I might even write you a poem."

She wrinkled her nose. "I don't need all that."

He eased her closer to him, moving his hands to her hips. "You do."

"I'm not that kind of woman." She waved in the direction of the driveway where the Cinderella carriage had taken Joanna to Bradford. "This is beautiful, but I didn't read about princesses as a child. I don't even see the practical reason for all these flowers. They're nice, but are they necessary?"

He leaned closer and kissed her forehead. Forehead. She was certain that wasn't a good sign. "Yes, and I'm going to show you why." He stepped back and took her hand in his. "Deal?"

She did want to be with him. "Deal."

He looked around the area, then said, "I'll be right back. I have something I need to do." Curious, she watched him go. He stopped to chat with people as he made his way through the crowd, but when his goal became clear, her mouth rounded in surprise.

Clay?

What does he need to speak to him about?

Oh, God. What did I just agree to?

Chapter Thirteen

A S DYLAN MADE his way through family and friends to the other side of the party he thought about what his father had said about him being a lot like his mother. He preferred to have time to think something over before he acted, but once he did he stayed the course.

When she'd described her past relationships, he'd imagined them too easily. He wondered if she realized how similar they sounded to her father. Why would someone do that to themselves? That was the question he'd asked himself.

Did she believe she didn't deserve better? That thought had made him sad.

When she'd suggested they have sex as a sort of test drive, he hadn't liked it. He might not be a pro at recognizing signs, but to him, that had been a clear one that if he didn't do something drastic she would begin to see him the same as her previous boyfriends.

Viviana had spent a good deal of their childhood encouraging the Sutton men to not only talk out their problems, but to listen to each other. Aly had already told him what she wanted. She'd also told him it wasn't easy for her. She'd let him in enough for him to understand that when she pulled away it was to protect herself from being hurt. Somewhere inside that beautiful, independent doctor was a little girl who still wondered if her father loved her.

He would bet his life the real reason she didn't buy into being romanced was because she didn't believe anyone could treasure her. If she went into a relationship with low expectations no one could disappoint her. That wasn't what he wanted their time together to be built on.

She deserves flowers, laughter, love from someone she can believe in. I want to give her that and so much more.

Even a strong woman needs a shoulder to lean on now and then. I can be that for her.

Not that Dylan was very experienced in the romance department, especially not lately. Finding female companionship hadn't been a struggle, even before he became an actor. He'd always been considerate to the women he'd dated, but he never put a lot of energy into maintaining those relationships.

This was different.

He wasn't ready to label it yet, but it felt important—like if he messed things up with Aly he just might spend the rest of his life regretting it. "Clay, can we talk?"

"Excuse me," Clay said to Asher and Ian Barrington. They looked curious but didn't ask what Dylan needed.

Once out of the earshot of others, Dylan said, "I'd like to hire you."

Clay laughed. "What?"

Okay, so that did sound improbable. "The Extraordinaire you."

"Oh." A huge smile spread across Clay's face. "There's no charge."

"Whew, because we both know I couldn't afford you."

"Too true." Clay looked across the tables toward Aly and waved. She tentatively raised a hand and waved back. "The two of you were looking pretty cozy, but when something matters it's best to bring in an expert."

"Clay—"

Clay gave him a quick once-over then sighed. "If you're asking if you need a makeover, I'd say yes. That shirt looks like something Connor would wear."

"It is. I found it in the trunk of his car. Little Sean threw—"

"No explanation needed. We'll look forward, not back."

"I don't need a makeover." He looked down. The shirt was more wrinkled than he'd realized, but it didn't stink . . . that had to count for something. "Focus for a minute, Clay."

Clay's eyebrows rose and he folded his arms across his chest. "I'm listening."

"I really like Aly."

Clay rolled his eyes. "Tell me something less obvious."

"I mean *really* like her. She might be the one."

"Now we're getting somewhere."

"She doesn't believe in romance, but I intend to change that."

Standing up straighter, Clay clapped his hands together once. "You'll need a private jet. Coffee in Paris, a boat ride for two in Vilnius, perhaps a little shopping in Marrakech.

Or would you prefer a private glass igloo in Kakslauttanen?"

"I don't want any of that."

"Wow, you've become high maintenance. I doubt you have to go that far to win this one over."

Dylan shook his head. "I'm talking about real romance—the kind you can't buy, the kind that lasts."

After a moment, Clay said, "I'm not sure what you want from me."

"Just listen to some of my ideas. Tell me if any sound better than the others."

"Oooookay."

"And I'm open to suggestions. Low-key things."

"Low key."

Dylan sighed. "If this doesn't work out I want it to be because she didn't want the *real* me."

"So when do we kidnap her father, duct tape him, and stick him in a laundry basket?"

Clay was a ballbuster, but Dylan liked that about him. "Tuesday?"

They shared a laugh.

A moment later, Clay said, "I'm in."

"I'm glad."

"I may sprinkle one or two little—"

"No, Clay."

"It will be so subtle you won't even notice." He glanced over at his wife. "Marriage has taught me a lot about women. I don't have to tell you to be good to Aly, because I know you will. But also keep her guessing. If she asks you what you're thinking, be vague. They never really want to know."

Dylan clapped Clay on the back. "See, you're already giving me helpful advice."

Clay's chest puffed at that. "I am." He looked at Dylan. "What's your first move?"

"Trying to not have sex with her."

"Interesting." Clay nodded. "Not where I would have started, but this is your plan."

ALY TRIED TO engage in conversation with a couple of her fellow guests, but her attention kept going back to Dylan. How much was he sharing with Clay and what was so damn funny?

Sophie Barrington appeared at her side. "I always did think you and Dylan would make a nice couple."

"Oh, we're not. A couple. Yet." She cleared her throat. "We—I don't know what we are."

Sophie smiled with all the understanding of a mother. "You'll figure it out."

Aly let out a shaky breath and kept her attention firmly planted on Sophie. "I'm sure we will." She had quickly become one of Aly's favorite people. She doted not only on her family, but also on those her children brought into her life.

"Dylan is such a good boy. He could use someone like you in his life."

"Like me?"

"Loyal. Supportive, but not a pushover. Sometimes a partner in crime, sometimes someone to bail him out."

Aly smiled. "I could use that as well."

"Dylan would be that as well." Sophie looked over to where he and Clay were still talking. "From the first time I met Dylan and Connor I knew I would love them as if they were my own. Connor had this way of swooping in, lifting me off my feet and twirling me around. Some thought he did it for the shock value, but that's how Connor lives—free and full on. Dylan would stand back and watch, wanting the same but careful to not offend. I never miss an opportunity to hug him because he needs it."

Dylan didn't come across as particularly sad or needy. "He's definitely more cautious than Connor."

Sophie sighed. "He took the loss of his mother hard, likely because he was older than Viviana and Connor. I'm so proud of the changes I've seen in him, but I adored him the way he was before as well. The Suttons are good people."

They were. It was interesting to hear Sophie's impression of Dylan. She saw straight to the heart of people, but did so with kind eyes. Having been raised without a mother, Aly had never had the guidance of an older female and her father had been far from nurturing. Sophie's warmth drew Aly to her.

Was my mother like Sophie? Who would I be today had she lived? Would relationships come easy to me or would I be just as closed off?

"Are you okay?" Sophie asked with concern.

When Aly's normal insistence that she was didn't feel right, she shrugged. "A little confused, that's all."

Sophie waited.

Aly continued, "Dylan told me he wants to take it slow

and *romance* me."

Sophie gasped and brought a hand to her chest. "That is so sweet."

"Except I'm not really the *romance* type."

Sophie gave her a long look. "Everyone is when it's done right." Her attention was drawn back to Dylan and Clay. "I do hope Clay doesn't fill his head with wild ideas of how that should look. I'll talk to them."

Aly grabbed Sophie's arm. "Oh, no, please don't. I shouldn't have said anything."

Sophie gave her hand a pat. "I can be quite subtle." She sighed. "Plus I feel a little responsible. I'm the one who started Clay down this whole Fairy Godfather road. I wanted him to feel included."

Aly looked over at Dylan and Clay and suddenly saw their exchange in a different light. Dylan liked Clay. He could be over there talking about anything. It didn't have to be about her. *I need to stop assuming that people are judging me.* "Does Clay ever talk about his family?"

"Not that I'm aware of. It breaks my heart. Family is everything and he seems so lost without his."

"He does." She wondered if he didn't have any or if he'd had a falling out with them.

"Speaking of family, we'd love to meet yours. Your father is welcome to join us for dinner any evening."

Every muscle in Aly's body tensed. "Thanks. I'll pass along the invite to him." *Or not.* Even if he meant well, her father had a way of taking the shine out of anything she shared with him.

"I'm sure you'll want to introduce Dylan to him first, but after that be sure to bring him by."

Introduce Dylan to him? Aly closed her eyes briefly. *Yeah, that's not happening anytime soon either.* Her father wouldn't have anything good to say about Dylan. Not that her father had ever approved of any of the men she'd dated. "One step at a time, Sophie. Dylan and I haven't even been on a date yet."

"That's not what I heard." Sophie made small swimming motions with her hands.

Aly's cheeks warmed. "How do you know about that?"

"Connor. When Angelina told him about it he thought it sounded like the perfect Icelandic outing, apparently she didn't." Sophie was smiling.

"I can't believe he—that little stinker. Remind me not to keep any of Connor's secrets."

Sophie laughed. "I doubt he has any."

True enough. Aly began to shoot Connor a glare, but when he caught her looking at him he waved and smiled and it was impossible to remain cross with him. His arm was around a glowing Angelina, who also smiled and waved. Aly waved back. "I can't even be upset with either of them. Look how happy they are."

After a moment, Sophie said, "Love does tend to have that effect on people."

Love. Great concept I've never come close to. Lust yes. Something deeper? For all I know I'm not even capable of it. Aly decided to change the topic. "Wasn't that a beautiful proposal? I'm so happy for Joanna and Bradford."

"It truly was. I'm sure yours will be just as special."

"Oh—I—we—" She stopped and smiled when she caught a sparkle in Sophie's eyes. "You like to get me all flustered about him."

Sophie winked. "I do. You often look so serious, I like to see you smile." She placed a hand on Aly's arm again. "My family has been growing exponentially lately—and I can't adequately express how happy that has made me. Whether you end up with Dylan or not, you'll always be welcome at our table."

Aly blinked a few times quickly then hugged her. "Thank you, Sophie. You have no idea how much that means to me."

Sophie stepped back and nodded toward Dylan. "I look forward to hearing what Dylan considers *romancing* you."

"I'll be sure to tell Angelina all about it so Connor can submit a detailed report." She was busting Sophie's chops this time.

Sophie laughed. "You do that."

As soon as Dylan started walking back to Aly, Sophie excused herself and met him halfway. Whatever she said to him made him duck his head and smile. She gave him that hug she said he needed then sent him on his way and continued on to where Clay was still standing.

For once she didn't worry what was being said. There was no one sweeter than Sophie. Aly met Dylan's gaze. She had no reason to doubt him either.

"Sorry," he said as he joined her. "That took longer than I meant it to."

Unable to help it, she asked, "What did Sophie say to you?"

He smiled down at her. "Nothing I didn't already know."

Vague. Frustrating. The success of her career depended on the quality of data she was able to collect regarding the health of a patient and the nature of their issue. Numbers. Facts. Documentable results. Those were the things she was most comfortable with.

If they really were moving forward in any sense, Aly wanted him to have the information he might require to make an informed decision. "I have trust issues. It's something I'm working on. I do trust you, but when you and Clay were laughing I felt—I was—"

"We did talk about you, but only in the best of ways." Dylan pulled her into his arms and hugged her to his chest. Against the side of her head he murmured, "You can trust me, Aly. I understand that it'll take time."

She tipped her head back and searched his face. "I do. That's why I'm being honest with you. Whatever we have feels important, and that scares me."

"Important. Yes, that's how this feels." He hugged her tighter. "I have faith, though, that we can figure this out—together."

Together. Partners in crime as well as each other's safety net. That was what had been missing in her prior relationships. *I never fully trusted them because we weren't on the same team.* Angelina was right, more wasn't possible until I lowered my guard. "When I said we could just have sex and see how it goes, that was the scared me talking. I was trying to prove to myself this wasn't different."

"But it is." His smile warmed every inch of her.

"Yes." She raised a hand to trace his strong jaw. "Thank you for not letting me ruin this before we've even given it a chance."

The look they shared was heated and paused time. He brushed his lips gently over hers in a brief kiss that left her shaken to the core. "You're welcome." With a groan, he set her back from him. "Let's go mingle before I forget today isn't about us."

Her body was humming and everything felt right with the world. He held out his hand and she laced her fingers through his without hesitation. *We're doing this.*

Chapter Fourteen

I T HADN'T BEEN easy to separate from Aly at the end of the engagement party. After sliding into the backseat of his brother's car next to his soon-to-be nephew, Whitney, Dylan sat back with a groan. The evening had gone so well. If she were any other woman they might already be rolling around in his bed.

She'd opened up to him about how hard it was for her to trust people and that she wasn't yet confident with him. Waiting wasn't an easy choice, but it was the right one.

"Are you dating Aly now?" Whitney asked and Dylan sat up straighter. He'd expected to be grilled by his brother, not Angelina's son.

"I think so."

"You don't know?" Angelina asked from the front seat. "You two looked like you'd finally figured it out."

"We did. I think. It's still a little up in the air."

Whitney frowned. "On your side or hers?"

His mother intervened. "Dylan, don't mind my son. Aly and Joanna practically raised him with me. He can be a little protective of them."

Whitney was an old soul in a young body. The next words out of his mouth might well be a threat to kick Dylan's ass if he messed up and it wouldn't be a joke. Damn, Dylan hoped his future kids had that level of grit. "It's a fair question. Mostly hers. I like her—a lot."

"Good." Whitney nodded. After a moment he said, "If you need any advice, just ask."

Dylan choked on a laugh he held back. "Thanks, I appreciate that."

"What were you talking to Clay about?" Connor asked.

Looking out the window at the passing scenery, Dylan considered how much he wanted to share. On one hand it was no one's business but his and Aly's, on the other—they were family. He hoped one day Whitney would come to him with relationship questions. "We just tossed some ideas around."

"About?" Angelina turned in her seat so she could face Dylan.

Dylan folded his arms over his chest. "I would tell you, but from what I hear secrets are not a thing to you."

Connor shrugged. "It's all Angelina's fault. She tells me everything."

With a laugh, Angelina shook her head. "We're a couple. I'm supposed to be able to tell you things, but that doesn't mean you have to repeat them."

Connor gave her a puppy-dog look. "When Sophie asks me questions she sees straight to my soul. It's like some kind of mind-meld I have no defense for."

"And Dad?" Dylan prodded.

"I can't lie to him," Connor said. "It's *Dad*."

"There's a difference between lying and vomiting my business all over everyone."

Connor looked into the rearview mirror and spoke to Whitney. "Dylan is nervous. If you weren't here he'd already be swearing and threatening to sock me in the head."

"I'm not nervous." Dylan crossed his arms over his chest.

Connor continued, "If I had to guess I bet talking about potential dates with Clay freaked him out and now he's second-guessing his ideas."

"Shut the—" Dylan stopped himself before swearing in front of his future sister-in-law. "I've never had a problem planning a date."

"Because blow-up dolls have low expectations."

Dylan leaned forward. "Do we need to pull the car over?"

Whitney laughed.

Angelina chuckled and covered her face with one hand. "Please don't."

They drove along a bit in silence. Eventually Whitney asked, "Dylan, *are* you nervous?"

Dylan gave him a look out of the corner of his eye. Lying offered the easiest path, but that wasn't what he wanted his relationship with Whitney to be based on. The kid was also smart as a whip. He might actually have a good idea. "A little." He glanced out the car window then back at Whitney. "I may have implied that I know how to be romantic. Aly is expecting me to wow her now. I was thinking simple was better, but after hearing Clay's suggestions I'm not so sure. I never had to put much effort into dating. What if Clay is right and I need to think bigger?"

Whitney shook his head. "I want to help, but I have no idea what women want."

From the front seat Connor said, "I am incredibly romantic and the proof is this lovely lady right next to me."

Dylan started to laugh and Whitney joined in. When Angelina burst out laughing as well, the three of them completely lost it.

"Hey," Connor said, "it's not that funny."

Angelina leaned over and put her head on his shoulder. "I love you just the way you are, Connor."

"I *am* romantic," Connor protested.

In a soothing tone, Angelina said, "Of course you are, hon." Then she looked over her shoulder and winked at Dylan and Whitney, throwing them both into another fit of laughter.

"You're all assholes," Connor said, but he was smiling. "I didn't hear you complaining, Angelina, when I took you on that shark encounter where it was just you and me in a steel cage with a great white circling."

"That's because I was so scared I was literally peeing in my wetsuit," Angelina said.

Whitney made a face that almost had Dylan laughing out loud again.

"Well no wonder the shark took off," Connor said. "No complaints about after the encounter?"

"No complaints about that," Angelina said, her voice becoming husky.

"Well, okay," Dylan said to Whitney. "What do you think if I start by calling her every night then take her to a nice restaurant this weekend?"

Whitney nodded then said, "She also likes butterflies. I remember her saying she went somewhere as a child and one landed on her hand. She loved it."

"That's actually helpful, Whitney." He leaned forward and clipped his brother in the back of the head again. "A shark encounter, really? Watch and learn, buddy. Whitney and I will show you how this is done."

A FEW HOURS later, Aly was fresh from a shower, already dressed in pajamas and tucked in her bed. Although she'd turned off the light, her eyes refused to shut. She was half expecting to wake up and realize the day had been nothing but a dream and she'd slept through her alarm.

I'm not asleep, though.

Today really happened.

She looked up at her ceiling and relived every moment of the party—from thinking Dylan was flirting with one of Joanna's staff to discovering what it was like to have Dylan at her side like they were a couple.

They'd eaten together, gone for a walk to see the horses, mingled with the Barringtons and Joanna's parents and snuck a few heated kisses along the way. Funny how something that had felt impossible when she'd woken up that morning suddenly wasn't.

She'd fully expected him to ask her to drive him home. Yes, he'd said he wanted to take things slowly, but their connection was so strong.

After giving her one brief kiss, he'd left her standing by her car, totally confused. All it took was one touch, one taste, for her to burn for him. What did it mean that he could make walking away look so easy?

She'd always felt sympathy for women who obviously cared more for their men than their men cared for them. She'd never imagined that might be her. Her desire for him defied logic, shattered everything she thought she understood about human sexuality. She was well versed on how a woman's body worked, the chemical reactions, even the health benefits of a good orgasm. What she was struggling to wrap her mind around was how strong her attraction to Dylan was. She'd wanted men before, but not like this.

She remembered reading an excerpt once from a romance and rolling her eyes. Sex was wonderful, but a person didn't *burn* for someone else.

Or so she'd thought. Breathless? Check. Unable to form a coherent sentence? Whenever he looks at me. *If he felt the same he'd be here with me, wouldn't he?*

Her phone rang. Dylan. She sat straight up and turned on the lamp beside her bed. "Hi."

"Hope it's not too late to call."

She didn't bother to check the clock. The time didn't matter. "No, not at all."

"I miss you already."

Whoosh, she melted back against her headboard. "I miss you too." She was tempted to tell him her address, but she wasn't looking for a repeat of their earlier conversation about waiting. Did he still want to wait? What would she say if he announced he'd changed his mind and asked to come over?

Um, hell, yes.

"I'm going to call you daily, Aly, unless you tell me it's too much. I'd like your voice to be the last thing I hear before I go to sleep."

She licked her bottom lip and closed her eyes. "I'd like that too."

"I'm going to do my best, but if it's too much or not enough, tell me."

"If what is too much?"

He didn't answer that question, but instead said, "My sister taught Connor and me a game when we were young. One person starts a sentence and the other finishes it."

"Like twenty questions? Should I think of an animal or color or something?"

"No, it's not that kind of game. It's about communication. Viviana was big on that when we were younger. She was always trying to get us to talk about our feelings."

"That's not at all how I was raised."

"I know," he said in a gentle tone. "So, let's try it. I'll start with an easy one. When I was little I wanted to be . . ."

"A doctor. I've always known. What about you?"

"An astronaut. It might have been all the sci-fi shows I watched where all the women were half dressed, though. I was kind of a horny kid."

Aly laughed. "Oh, boy. Okay. Something most people don't know about me is . . ."

"I don't like violence—at all. I hate when I see someone

doling it out, I hate when it's where I have to go to stop it. I'd always rather talk it out. Except with Connor. He knows all my buttons and he gives as good as he gets. What about you?"

"I've never hit anyone in my life."

"Never?"

"Never." She tucked an arm under her head. "Don't get me wrong, I've been tempted to, but I haven't allowed myself to."

"Have you ever tried kickboxing?"

"No."

"I bet you'd love it. Want to try it together sometime?"

"I'd love to."

"My turn. I love my life, but . . ."

"Sometimes I get lonely." *Did I really just say that? Oh, my God, how pathetic is that?*

"Me too."

She scoffed at that. "I doubt that. You have women following you around everywhere."

"You don't have to be alone to feel lonely. I went from living in the same house as my family in a town where I knew everyone's name. Now I have apartments in different cities where I can walk around for days without seeing a familiar face. Too much time in a city makes me homesick. When that happens, I fly home to visit my dad and he always says something that makes me feel better."

Aly sighed. "That's beautiful. And not at all the relationship I have with my father. I have to be in an exceptionally good mood when I see him, and even then I'll leave feeling a little—shredded."

"That's a shame. Have you ever told him that?"

She shook her head. "You don't know my father. If I tried to talk to him about how I felt it would only annoy him."

Dylan didn't speak for a moment then said, "I'm sorry."

"Don't be. That's who he is. Enough about him, it's my turn. It's not something I need, but I'd like . . ."

"To see you on Saturday."

Aly fanned her face as her mind took that innocent request to all kinds of naughty directions. "Funny, that's what I'd like as well."

"I'm planning a little surprise for you. It was actually Whitney's idea."

Huh? "Whitney? As in Angelina's son?" They were definitely not imagining the same kind of date. The kid was a soccer fanatic. "Is this where I should remind you I'm not athletic?"

"Oh, damn, then I need to rethink the whole date." He laughed. "No, wait, I knew that."

An unsettling thought came to her and she voiced it. "I've always hated sports."

"But you were on a swim team."

"Exactly."

"Gotcha."

"I like to hike, but I'm not into running, so if you're hoping that will change, it will not. Yoga stresses me out. And my favorite part about lifting weights is putting them down."

"Aly."

"Yes?"

"I don't look at you and see a single thing I would change." His tone lightened. "And I'm damn near perfect, so we should be good."

She chuckled. "What size is the pillow you lay that ego of yours on each night?"

"Did no one ever tell you it's rude to ask a man about his size?"

"I wasn't referring . . ." She rolled her eyes and laughed again. Had anyone ever made her laugh as easily as he did? She grimaced as she thought about her initial impression of him and how wrong it had been. What had he thought of her? "When we first met, I thought you were . . ."

"Brilliant," he said without hesitation. "Loyal. Beautiful."

She felt even worse because she knew he was sincere.

He asked, "How about you?"

She didn't answer at first. There was honest and then there were unnecessary truths.

He laughed. "That bad?"

"I thought you were attractive."

"But?"

"But—" *Oh, what the hell.* "I didn't think you'd be able to handle my career." He was quiet after that and she regretted not lying. "All I knew were the stories I'd heard."

Still nothing.

He'd been so good to her and how did she reward that? Right out of the gate she had to be a jerk. "Dylan, I'm so sorry. I didn't know you."

"You still don't," he said in a firm tone. Then his voice filled with humor. "Because I'm totally fucking with you. Relax, I know people used to call Connor and me meatheads. I'm not surprised you had that impression of me as well. I did my share to earn that title. The important part is you did think I was hot, right?"

All her tension ebbed right out of her. He was steady like a mountain and it calmed the storm in her. "You're an ass. I felt bad."

"You should have, but you know what would make it up to me? One hell of a kiss when I pick you up on Saturday."

She found herself smiling at the ceiling. Saturday felt like a lifetime away, but there was also something incredible about savoring this stage. "I might be able to arrange that."

"Might? I'll have to up my game."

IF ANYONE HAD asked Dylan how long he would want to be on the phone with anyone, he would have said he was more of a text guy. Talking? That was best done around a campfire with a few beers. Or while fishing. He'd once had a decent extended conversation while up on a hot air balloon ride, because really what else was there to do up there? Surprisingly, though, he could talk to Aly for hours. In fact, the more they spoke, the more he was convinced every relationship should start on the phone. He hadn't realized until just then that most prior dates had been more about doing something or doing each other than getting to know each other.

The question for him had been how to make a nightly phone call "romantic." Clay and Whitney had both given conflicting advice. Clay believed the bigger the gift the better. Go big or go home. Whitney suggested thoughtful gifts made a more powerful impact. After thinking it over, Dylan decided the best course for him lay somewhere in the middle.

The next morning he had high-tech boxing equipment delivered to his apartment as well as hers. When he called her that evening she was concerned that he hadn't understood when she said she wasn't athletic. However, once they both put on their boxing gloves and connected the devices online they became avatars on their television screens and laughed their way through beating the crap out of each other.

Aly might claim not to be competitive, but she gave as good as she got. Afterward, they both grabbed bottles of water and collapsed onto their couches for a video chat.

"That was actually a lot of fun," she said with a beautiful all-over glow.

"Maybe because I have a little sister, but I'm a big advocate of women knowing how to land a good kick. Plus, if you have a bad day you can always tape someone's face to the bag."

She laughed at that. That night they talked until almost midnight. She told him about how she'd met Joanna and Angelina in college and how they'd instantly just clicked. The next day Dylan called Angelina first thing in the morning and asked her to locate a photo of the three of them in college—specifically one Aly might not have already. Angelina sent him one of the three of them, arms around each other, smiling into the camera. He had it printed, framed and delivered to Aly at her job.

That night, Aly's voice was husky when she greeted him. "Thank you so much for the photo, Dylan. I hung it in my office. Really, that was probably the most considerate gift anyone has ever given me."

It was exactly what he'd hoped to hear. He hated the idea that in the past she'd chosen men who hadn't made her feel special.

Their conversation that evening took them all the way back to childhood. Hers had been a lonely one. It didn't sound as if her father had been abusive, nor had he been aware that his daughter had needed more of him than he'd given her. She'd never been hungry, never gone without what she needed. He'd made sure she was well educated and socially responsible. Not a bad man, but definitely not a nurturer.

On the outside Aly might look self-sufficient and not at all in need of pampering, but there was a softer side to her . . . one that reminded him of himself. He understood how easily the expectations of a parent could shape a child.

His father had needed him to be strong for the sake of his younger siblings. He shared with Aly how after his mother's funeral, his father had told him he needed to stop crying because he was scaring Connor. He told Aly about how his father had echoed his mother's dying wish that he look after his siblings. From then on, until Viviana met Grant Barrington, Dylan had been the man his family needed him to be and so much so that he'd lost touch with what he'd wanted for himself.

Aly said she understood. Her father had kept an immaculate, quiet house. By sheer habit, Aly was also meticulously clean, but every now and then she deliberately left a dirty dish out in her apartment. She lived alone so it bothered no one, but it was her own little rebellion. "Sometimes I even blare my music."

"No," Dylan had said in a dry tone. "Aren't you concerned about your neighbors?"

"I only do it during the day."

He laughed, realized she was serious, and cleared his throat. "It feels good to cut loose now and then."

"It does. The guy downstairs has parties during the week and is so loud I have to wear headphones to sleep."

The next day Dylan sent her an expensive set of speakers, an empty pizza box, and one sock. She was still laughing when she called him via video chat to thank him. They blasted music and sang along until her downstairs neighbor banged on the ceiling, then they blasted the music louder and sang some more.

Later, with a smile, she held up the sock and asked, "What exactly am I supposed to do with this?"

"Put it in the middle of the floor."

"I can't."

"You can. Try it. Just take it and fling it then let it lie wherever it lands."

"Is it even clean?"

He shrugged. "Don't ask questions you don't want the answer to."

She shuddered. "I can't believe I'm doing this." With that, she twirled it over her head and let it fly. "Oh, my God, you're not going to believe it, it landed on a photo of my father." She laughed until she was wiping tears from the corner of her eyes. "I can't leave it there."

Dylan shrugged. "One night with a smelly sock never hurt anyone."

"And the pizza box?"

"Leave it on the couch. Or the floor. Really, anywhere. It's a statement piece."

"We can never tell anyone we did this."

Although she was still smiling, he didn't love that she wasn't entirely joking. Despite being an accomplished doctor in her own right, she didn't feel like she could challenge him and that made Dylan a little sad. He respected his own father, but he wasn't afraid to disagree with him. He hoped Aly would one day find that same sense of security with her father.

On Wednesday he sent her a puzzle of her favorite flower and a bottle of wine. They each drank a glass and worked on it together remotely. Putting a puzzle together via video chat required compromise but that was what made it so interesting. They had the same goal but different strategies. It was a push and pull exercise in the beginning until they found a comfortable middle ground where they meshed their two styles. She sorted by color the way she liked to but then started with the outer edge the way he was comfortable. After placing the last piece in, she said, "I've never built a puzzle with anyone before."

"And?"

"It was wonderful." Her smile nearly had him sprinting for his car and rushing over to her place. He told himself to be patient and that this was every bit as important as where it was leading to. Her eyes misted over. "Dylan, everything you've done and sent this week has been great, but I'm beginning to feel guilty. I want to send you something but I have no idea what you like."

He told her not to worry about it, but the next day he sent her a journal entitled, "Things I could give Dylan that would make him happy." It had taken him a while to fill it out, but he'd written on each page. He alternated sweet or practical choices and sexual suggestions. If she actually read it she would not only know his favorite teams, foods, colognes, and tool brands but she'd also have insight into a few of his kinks. He even listed some of his favorite positions. When he didn't know a quick term for it he made a little stick person sketch.

When she didn't immediately call him to say she'd received it, he worried that he might have gone too far. He'd meant it to be lighthearted and fun, but keeping on the theme of getting to know each other. His concern, though, was that he should've heeded Clay's warning about remaining vague. He called her but she didn't answer. He texted and still nothing. Not good.

He was still debating if he should drive over to her place and apologize when a courier delivered the journal back to him. He groaned and gave himself a mental kick in the ass for ruining what had been a great week.

Then he saw the note attached to it.

Your preferences have been noted. Please refer to my notes for feedback. –Aly.

She'd taken the time to write on each and every page. A grin spread across his face as he went through her responses. She wasn't into football, but she was a fan of the same hockey team he was. More importantly, she'd put hearts next to all the things they both liked to do in bed. Okay, so there were one or two she wasn't as into, but he did appreciate the additions she wrote in.

On one of his diagrams she wrote she was willing to try it but she wasn't sure it was humanly possible. He burst out laughing. She'd apparently only been with weak men. By the end of the book he wasn't afraid to admit to himself that he was falling in love with her.

He called her and although he was tempted to indulge in one of the activities she said she liked, he wanted to wait for their date so he thanked her for her notes and pretended he wasn't going to reread them a hundred times and treasure that book for fucking forever.

On Friday he sent her a large wrapped box and asked her not to open it until after their date the next day. She sent him a signed football from his favorite player. As they chatted that night, the anticipation of seeing her again was excruciating in the most wonderful way.

He'd never wanted a woman more.

Or felt he knew one as well.

The only difficult part of their date would be holding to his plan and not carrying her off and pounding into her on the nearest bed, or stairway, or wall. If the universe was just at all, their date would start with her feeling the same way.

And end with several checkmarks in that journal.

Chapter Fifteen

FIRST DATES DIDN'T make Aly nervous.

Scratch that, before Dylan, no first date had ever made her nervous. She was a tangled mess of anxiety by the time she slid into the passenger seat of his car that Saturday afternoon. Dylan had refused to tell her where they were headed. The only hint he'd given her was to dress casual and wear walking shoes.

She felt like she'd started off their date on an awkward note. When he'd come to her door she'd wanted to throw herself in his arms, but hesitated and just said, "Hey."

It was a lame greeting and didn't represent how she felt at all, but he'd said he wanted to take things slowly, and so far that was proving to be amazing. She didn't want to do anything to mess it up. So, she attempted to take her cue from him, but he looked more concerned than physically excited and that only confused her more.

She'd expected a kiss, definitely at least a hug. Instead he ducked his head down closer to hers and said, "Hey, yourself. You ready?"

She'd let out a shaky breath. "Absolutely."

He didn't take her hand on the way down to the car and that had her doing mental somersaults as she tried to figure out why. Every phone conversation they'd had had been more magical than the one before. They'd ended the one they'd had the night before by saying they couldn't wait to see each other in person. What had changed? Aly clasped her hands on her lap and warned herself to calm down before she ruined the entire date.

"Breathe," he said after climbing into the driver's seat. "It's just me, Aly."

She forced herself to meet his gaze. "I know."

He gave her a funny look. "So talk to me. What are you worried will happen today?"

Her hands fisted on her lap as she tried to figure that out for herself. "This week was so perfect."

He placed his hand over one of hers. "It was."

"I don't want to ruin it."

Lifting one of her fisted hands in his, he brought it to his lips. "You could only do that if you didn't show up."

She searched his face. "Why am I so nervous?"

He chuckled. "You're not the only one. Hell, I'm taking a brilliant doctor out on a first date. Do you think I'm not asking myself if I chose the right place? If I went too far or not far enough?"

Her hand relaxed in his and their fingers laced together. "You think that's bad? I'm going on a date with a guy who might possibly be the most considerate man on the planet. I told him I didn't believe in romance and now I have to tell him I was wrong—it's actually pretty wonderful."

"Is that the same man who sprinted down to his car with you because he was afraid if he kissed you at your door the date would never happen?"

His smile warmed every inch of her. "I do believe it might be."

He took her hand and laid it on his thigh, high enough to start her heart racing. God, he had the kind of muscular thighs fantasies were built around. "Then those two belong together because they both sound fucking neurotic to me."

When he started the car, she joked, "I hear she's having a complete breakdown. Rumor is her living room is full of empty pizza boxes, dirty socks, puzzle pieces and workout equipment."

"But is she happy?"

Without missing a beat, she answered, "More than she's been in a very long time."

"That's all that matters, then."

Aly had never been in love, but there was no other word that fit how she felt. Lust for him had been replaced by something much deeper. It was hard to remember life before him or to imagine life without him now. She tightened her hand on his thigh. "I'm not even sure I deserve someone as nice as you are."

He pulled the car over and turned in his seat. "Viviana took a psychology class one year and she came back with some strange ideas, but one thing she said stuck with me. She said we all have voices in our heads, like a recording we're sometimes not even aware is playing in the background. If we listen to it and it's not saying nice things, we need to rerecord what we say to ourselves. I didn't fully understand it, but I think what you just said is what is playing in the background of your head. You do deserve to be treated well. Everyone does."

Fighting back embarrassment, she hugged her arms around herself. "I know that."

He touched one of her temples lightly. "You know it here." Then he ran a hand down her neck to her heart, just above the curve of her breast. "But you don't here. Maybe here is where the recording comes from."

Tears filled her eyes but she blinked them back.

He reached up to caress her cheek. "Repeat after me: I'm a good person and I deserve good things in my life."

When she didn't parrot his words, he arched an eyebrow and waited. Although she felt a little silly, she hadn't liked what had come out of her mouth any more than he had. It didn't fit how she saw herself. So, what the hell . . . "I'm a good person and I deserve good things in my life."

"I deserve respect."

"I deserve respect."

"I deserve patience when I'm not perfect."

"I deserve patience when I'm not perfect."

"Dylan Sutton is a sex god."

Aly barked out a laugh and he shrugged. Smiling, she said, "Dylan Sutton may be a sex god. I can't really say until I have some empirical evidence."

"Is that the kind of evidence that requires experimentation?"

"It is."

"Yes." He pumped his fist in the air. "High school science projects were not a waste of time. See, I learned something."

They shared another laugh, then the mood between them turned more serious. She placed her hand on his thigh again and said, "You're right about that recording, Dylan, and I do need to change it. I don't know if that's my voice or my father's but I need to get it out of my head."

He leaned over and kissed her gently. Passion burned just beneath the surface of that kiss, but it was an emotionally charged exchange as well. "My father would call it noise you can learn to tune out."

She nodded. "Thank you."

He sat back and pulled out into traffic again. They drove along for a few minutes in comfortable silence, then he said, "If you're really grateful you can always move your hand a little higher."

She laughed and did just that. Running her hand back and forth over his cock as it hardened beneath his jeans was sweet torture but one she knew he enjoyed just as much.

BY THE TIME they arrived at their destination his jeans were an uncomfortable containment device to the point where he had to remove her hand and ask for a few minutes before they got out of the car. He was half cursing himself for choosing such a public place to take her to, but if he could get any of the blood that had settled in his crotch to return to his head he knew she'd enjoy what he'd planned.

Holy shit.

He closed his eyes and tried to remember the name of every MVP in Superbowls in his lifetime. It was a trick he'd come up with in middle school when his erections had seemed to not only have a mind of their own, but also horrible timing.

"Are you okay?" she asked.

He raised a hand. "One more minute."

"I'm sorry."

He opened his eyes. "I'm not. The only mistake I made was in timing. I'm good now, though. Let's go."

She tilted her head to one side then seemed to change her mind about what to say. "Where are we?"

"It's a butterfly park. Whitney said you told him you once had one land on your hand and it was something you loved."

"I did and it was." Her mouth rounded. "I forgot I even told Whitney about that." She undid her seat belt and turned toward Dylan. Could this be real? Was it how things were supposed to be? *If it feels too good to be true—*

She stopped herself there. *That's the voice.*

Everyone had their own version of it. Easy to spot in others, uncomfortable to acknowledge in oneself. Joanna was stronger than those who doubted Bradford, and she found love. Angelina let herself finally trust someone again and that made what she had with Connor possible.

Dylan had called it noise. Yes, that's what it was. *And I refuse to listen to it anymore.*

"Am I missing something?" Dylan asked. "You look—"

She leaned over and kissed him then and let her mouth

and tongue express how grateful she was that he'd come into her life. She moaned and deepened the kiss, hoping it made her feelings for him clear.

When she sat back his face was flushed, he looked a little shaken, and he raised one finger in the air. "I'm going to need another moment."

She leaned over and whispered in his ear playfully, "I'm not sorry this time."

Grinning from ear to ear, he said, "Get your ass out of this car, but hold that thought for later."

They met in front of the car and linked hands. Only once they were inside the park did Aly see a sign guiding them toward the butterfly pavilion. She quickened her step without realizing it and Dylan sped up to keep pace with her. "I had no idea this place was here."

"I was hoping you hadn't been here. The reviews were good, but it's a little out of the way so I took a chance."

The pavilion was a large netted area with a double-gated entrance. As they entered they were handed a laminated sheet with photos of all types of butterflies they might see. The place was surprisingly empty. They followed a path that was flanked on both sides with flowering plants. At first it felt as if there were an overwhelming number of butterflies, too many to isolate and identify. However, as they slowed their pace Aly began to appreciate the beauty of one type at a time.

A giant swallowtail flew and landed right in the middle of Dylan's chest. He stopped and turned toward her. She laid her hand on his chest beside it, marveling more at the heavy thud of his heartbeat than the butterfly. She'd never met such a kindhearted man and she doubted she ever would again. The butterfly crawled up onto her fingers.

"He likes you," Dylan said. "He has excellent taste."

"I wonder how you can tell if it's a male or female."

Dylan winked. "And I thought you were an expert on such things."

She laughed and the butterfly flew away, but she left her hand where it was. "I always knew the jokes would come, but strangely enough, I don't mind them."

He pulled her closer and gave her a kiss so sweet she nearly forgot where they were. She ran her hands up his strong back and moved against him.

"Excuse me," an attendant said.

They broke off the kiss and turned to address him.

The young man asked, "Mr. Sutton?"

"That's me," Dylan answered.

"There's a bench in the next area if you'd like to take a seat."

"Thanks," Dylan said, "but we're fine."

"You should at least go look at it," the young man insisted.

Aly glanced at Dylan. He looked as confused as she was. They thanked the man and walked into the next area.

There on the side was an ornate bench. They stepped closer. Aly read aloud the plaque on it. "'Dedicated to all those on first dates. May they experience as much wonder and transformation as the beautifully winged angels housed here.' It has our names and today's date." Aly's jaw dropped open. "You did this?"

Dylan made a pained face. "Yes and no. I planned the date and I may have mentioned it to Clay. The bench is his idea of sprinkling magic. Too much?"

Aly gave him a full body hug. "No, it's perfect." It was concrete evidence that she wasn't imagining what was happening between them. She closed her eyes and took a leap of faith. "Wouldn't it be amazing to come back next year and sit here?"

He enveloped her in a hug and kissed her forehead. "And the year after."

She shuddered against him as waves of fear and love and desire crashed through her. "Yes." She said that word like a vow.

Neither of them spoke for several moments after that. They sat on the bench, holding hands, breathing each other in, staring into each other's eyes. It was an experience she would never forget. Intense. Vivid. Full of promise. Finally, he cleared his throat and said, "Well, okay, let's see what's in the next area."

They walked from one part of the pavilion to the next. If there were butterflies, she didn't notice. All of her senses were tuned to the man beside her. By the time they left the building and returned to his car, the sexual tension between them was nearly unbearable.

They buckled in and pulled out of the parking lot in record time. She slid her hand up his thigh and cupped his bulging cock. There was no longer any doubt in her. As he drove she undid his belt, unsnapped and unzipped his jeans.

Her body was pulsing with need for him and she licked her lips. "I noticed oral sex was written more than once in your journal. You didn't specifically mention if you like to come while you drive."

"Oh, God yes," he groaned and shifted so she would have better access to his huge and fully erect cock.

She released her seat belt and bent over him, taking him deeply in her mouth while cupping his shaven balls with one hand. There were areas of her life where she was less confident, but sex had never been one of them. In her studies she'd not only made it a point to understand the female body, but the male's as well.

Up and down, deeper and deeper, all the time seeking out his favorite moves. She brought him to the edge of orgasm and stopped, brought him there again and did the same. He was wild for release by the time he pulled over onto a side road and dug his hands into her hair.

She drank him in then undid the top of her jeans and guided his hand to her wet sex. "You think you can make me come while you drive?" she asked.

His finger sought out her clit and began to move slowly back and forth over it. "I hope I don't run anyone over, but I'm willing to try."

He started driving again and as he did he began to do the most incredible things with his fingers. No one was killed in the process but they did need to pull over one more time before they made it to her place. Apparently announcing she was close to coming meant two hands would be required. She had no complaints about that decision.

A few minutes later, looking disheveled and like they'd both dressed hastily in the car, they practically sprinted from her parking garage to her apartment. Once inside, clothing flew in all directions. His kisses were hot and demanding, his hands strong and worshipping. Against the inside of the door of her apartment he lifted her, swung her legs over his shoulders and buried his face in her sex. She braced herself against the wall as his thick tongue teased her already engorged clit then delved inside her, withdrew, and repeated the sweet move. His grip on her ass was forceful, his tongue relentless. It was the ultimate trust exercise. She was high off the ground and relying completely on him both for pleasure and for safety. She wasn't one who gave up control easily, but as a tsunami of an orgasm rose within her, she gave herself over to the pleasure of it and to him.

She cried out his name.

Cursed at him.

Begged him not to stop.

When she came it was like nothing she'd experienced before. She would have sworn on her life she'd levitated. She was still shaking, still breathing raggedly when he slid her down slowly, taking his time to claim each of her breasts with his mouth before settling her onto his sheathed, rock-hard cock. As he slid inside, she widened her legs, and wrapped them around his waist. God, he was so big . . . all of him. She adjusted herself to take him deeper.

Then came his first thrust. Powerful. Primal. She gasped from how he filled her. There was no gentleness in him, nor did she want any. She was his for the taking, and man, did he know how to take.

Against the wall of her apartment, still just inside the door, he pounded into her. Harder. Deeper. Faster. Again and again until she wasn't sure she could take anymore. He slowed and kissed her almost tenderly as his hands did the most deliciously pain/pleasure things to her nipples until she was writhing wildly against him, demanding more.

More came with powerful thrusts that took them both to a sweaty, gloriously spent place. He lowered her to her feet, cleaned himself off, then returned and smiled down at her. "So this is your place. Nice."

Still leaning against the wall, she said, "If you think this is good, you should see the rest of it."

"I intend to." He leaned down and claimed her mouth again with a bold tongue then grinned down at her.

She could barely breathe as she looked up at him. *I want this man . . . in my life, in my bed, in my future.* The intensity of the moment was almost too much to bear so she joked, "Now that I know how strong you are, I may have to add a few sketches to that journal."

"Sketch away." He laughed and lifted her into his arms, carrying her across the living room of her apartment. "Which way to your bedroom?"

She pointed toward a hallway and joked, "It's so far. Think we'll make it?"

"Possibly." He stopped, bent to kiss her neck, then flick his tongue across one of her nipples.

They didn't. One touch led to another until he was on the carpeted floor, she was on top, and they discovered he was perfectly content to let her take control as well.

A FEW HOURS later, tucked into Aly's bed with her asleep at his side, Dylan acknowledged that as far as first dates went, this had by far been the best. Was it their first? It certainly didn't feel that way. Every moment they'd been together felt significant.

He wanted to wake her up and tell her right then and there that they were meant to be and that this was forever. He didn't because he didn't want to see her bolt for the door, but he'd never been more certain about anything in his life.

This was his woman.

For good. For bad. For life. He was where he wanted to be. As he ran a hand gently up and down Aly's back, he thought about things his father had said over the years. He remembered talking to his father about if he ever imagined himself married again. His father said he couldn't because no one would ever compare. It had sounded sweet to Dylan and he'd liked that his mother had been that important to his father, but he hadn't fully understood what he'd meant until Aly.

There might have been other women who were as intelligent, as beautiful, even as snarky as she was—but none had ever touched his heart the way Aly did. He felt connected to her, in tune with her emotions in a way he hadn't imagined possible for him.

Her eyes fluttered and opened. "Hi, handsome."

"Hey, Doc."

She yawned, stretching her bare body along his. Heaven. "What time is it?"

"No idea, but it's still dark so it's safe to say it's early. Do you have anywhere you need to be today?"

She ran a hand across his chest. "No, you?"

He nuzzled her neck. "No, but I can't imagine plans I wouldn't cancel to stay right here."

She shifted so even more of her body was touching his. "Right here?" Her hand wandered down his stomach to encircle his cock that was already hardening in anticipation. "Or *here*?"

He rolled so he was braced on his elbows above her and settled himself between her legs. By raising and lowering his hips he moved his cock back and forth over her sex, slipping it more between her folds each time. His kiss was warm and leisurely, she was wet and ready. He slid his cock in slowly and rotated his hips until she moaned and whispered, "That's the spot."

He took his time, keeping each entry controlled. He gently rocked his hips while their kisses deepened. Her hands were everywhere and she tightened and released herself on his cock in a way that had him nearly out of his mind, but he didn't want to rush.

He waited for her breathing to change, for her chest to flush and those gorgeous eyes of hers to begin to close as she approached release . . . only then did he let himself increase speed and pound down into her.

She cried out his name, clawed at his back.

He drove himself deeper and deeper into her and

growled. "Right here. This is where I want to spend the day." He came with one final thrust.

"Oh, yes," she sobbed as she joined him.

They remained joined as they came back to earth. He tucked a stray hair behind her ear and kissed still parted lips. "Sex god?" he joked.

Still breathing raggedly, she wrapped her arms around his neck and said, "I'm still gathering data. It might be an extensive process."

He chuckled. "I don't have a problem with that."

She looked away for a moment, then met his gaze again. "Seriously, this was good, Dylan. Amazing. It normally isn't like this for me."

"You think it is for me?" When she didn't immediately answer, he realized she needed more. "This is all new for me. I've been with more women than my mother would have approved of, but I've never been with someone I could picture waking up with every day." He withdrew from her and rolled onto his side. "I'm going to say something that might freak you the fuck out, but I think you need to hear it. I'm all in, falling hard and fast. I see us married, raising kids together, fighting over who forgot to pay the electricity bill."

Her eyes rounded and she looked a lot like a deer frozen in headlights. "I've never forgotten to pay a bill."

That made him smile. He pulled her closer and kissed the tip of her nose. "Then we'll be fine."

She blinked several times fast. "You love me?"

"Like I said . . . falling hard and fast."

She sat straight up and took several deep breaths. "What

you're experiencing could be the chemical afterglow of good sex."

"Breathe." He moved to put an arm around her. "Aly, you don't have to be on the same page yet, but it's important to me that you know how I feel. For me, this is the real deal."

She shook beneath his arm. "Could I have a moment?"

He moved back. "Sure."

She scooted off the bed and bolted out of the room. It wasn't the ideal response, but not unexpected. He didn't regret telling her, even if she needed time to process it. Love shouldn't be about playing games or torturing each other. Aly needed a rock and that's what he wanted to be for her.

If that meant he needed to be the one to risk more, trust first . . . she was worth it.

Chapter Sixteen

ALY HUGGED HERSELF as she paced the living room. She was angry with herself for running, angry with him for being too much too soon. Did he expect her to announce she loved him? Just like that?

Her gaze fell on the piles of their clothing that were still strewn near the door. She walked over, picked up his large shirt and hugged it to her bare chest. *I'm not angry. I'm scared.*

Why couldn't I just kiss him back and tell him I'm all in as well? What's wrong with me?

He sees a future with me—one with kids and shared vows.

I want that too. She slid his shirt over her head and smiled absently at how long it was on her. He was a big guy, not just physically, but with an equally big heart. He was everything she was just beginning to understand she'd always wanted. *And that's terrifying.*

She took several deep breaths and prayed he hadn't followed her yet. She kept going over what he'd said and each time she did she panicked a little less. He wasn't the type who would demand she change for him. He was a good man.

Solid.

She stopped her internal dialogue before it could add, "Better than I deserve."

As a doctor, she believed in diagnosing a health issue and then facing it head-on. What she was discovering was that mental issues were trickier. She felt each time she took a step forward she slid two back.

Dylan just said he's falling in love with me and I'm hiding from him. This. This is what I need to fix.

What am I so afraid of?

That he doesn't mean it? He has no reason to lie and he's done nothing to make me think he would.

Why do I believe I can't find love the way my friends did?

What the hell do I think is so wrong with me?

Out of the corner of her eye she caught a glimpse of the large present Dylan had sent and asked her not to open before their date. She walked over and ran her hand tentatively over it.

She'd reluctantly agreed to being romanced. Presents and flowers had always sounded like wasted effort to her—until they came from Dylan. He'd used them to show her that he saw her, heard her, wanted her to be happy. In different ways each present had opened her heart a little more to him.

What would he have sent over in a box big enough that it might house a small piece of furniture? And why had he wanted her to wait?

There was a card attached to one side of it. She held it out in front of her for a long moment before opening it. It was handwritten in simple, strong lettering that was classic

Dylan.

Aly,

You're an early morning sunrise
A laugh so hard I fart
A smile I can't contain
An overflowing shopping cart

You're a rash that finally fades
A twenty-dollar bill found on the ground
You're a tie during extra innings
Something lost, missed, and then found

I never thought I could feel this way
Never thought it would be you
But you can have my heart
And if you want it
Everything below that too.

Love,
Dylan

In a mixture of laughter and tears, Aly reread the poem. It was perfectly him. Funny. Heartfelt. Loving. She folded it up and put it on the table beside the box.

With much less patience she tore away the wrapping paper and gasped as his gift was revealed. It looked like a white bird cage on a stand but instead of bars it had clear plexiglass. The interior sides were covered with small flowering plants. On the floor of it was a plastic container that looked like it held caterpillars on some kind of gel food source.

Butterflies.

It's a butterfly habitat.

There was a tiny card inside next to the plastic container.

Aly's first pet.

She brought a shaking hand to her mouth. It was a perfect gift from a perfect man. She turned and strode back toward the bedroom to thank him. If he was upset with her she would do her best to explain that her panic had nothing to do with how she felt about him. Just outside the bedroom door she took a deep fortifying breath and told herself that even if he was a little defensive at first, she would wait it out and show him that she was worth forgiving.

The sound of snoring greeted her as soon as she opened the door. Dylan was sound asleep. Was he upset at all?

She sat on the edge of the bed. "Dylan?"

One of his eyes opened a little and the snoring ceased. "Yes?"

"You're sleeping."

"I was."

"Weren't you worried about me?"

"You said you needed a minute." His voice was still thick from sleep. "Did you want me out there?"

"No."

"That's what I thought." He yawned. "You okay?"

"Yes." *I think.* "I read your note and opened your present. Both were beautiful. Thank you."

He smiled. "You're welcome. I'm glad you liked them."

"Dylan?"

"Yeah?"

Deep breath. *I just need to say it. I can do this.* "I love you."

He held up an arm. "I know. Get over here."

She ditched the shirt and slid beneath the covers and into his arms. He hugged her from behind and kissed her neck.

Could love really be that easy? "Dylan?"

"Mmmm?" he asked against her hair.

"Could you say it?"

"That I love you?"

Oh, God, I'm an idiot. "Forget it."

He rolled her over so they were face-to-face. "Aly, I have no problem saying it. I've been saying it all week, just not in words. I love you."

She searched his face. "I believe you. I don't know why I get so scared sometimes."

He pulled her to his chest and tucked her beneath his chin. "You'll feel better after you introduce me to your father."

She tensed in his arms and her voice came out as a squeak. "My father?"

"It's the natural next step." He kissed her forehead. "You're worried it won't go well, but have a little faith in me."

She nodded even though she couldn't shake the sense of dread that had descended on her. She was just beginning to build herself up. She wasn't ready to take Dylan to meet the only man capable of tearing her down.

Chapter Seventeen

A COUPLE OF weeks later Dylan was standing in the middle of Sophie and Dale's living room, flapping his arms. He'd never been a fan of charades, but the Barringtons gathered weekly for game night and he and Connor tried to join in at least once a month. It was a great way to see not only them, but his father and sister as well.

His team that week consisted of Aly, Viviana, Grant, Dale, and Whitney. They'd correctly guessed that he was acting out a movie title, but he couldn't get them away from the word bird.

"Lady Bird," Viviana called out.

Dale guessed. "Bird on a Wire."

"Big Bird," Grant added.

Dylan shook his head, brought his feet together and waddled.

"Howard the Duck," Aly guessed.

Whitney joined in with, "Mighty Ducks."

Dylan frowned, made a circle with his hands to represent an egg, then put it behind him and pretended to sit on it. They all stopped guessing and gave him an odd look like he'd lost them.

"Time's up," Asher Barrington called out. "Looks like we win again."

Laughing Connor interjected, "You lost us when you did the turd thing at the end."

Dylan gladly returned to his spot beside Aly on one of the couches. "It was *The March of Penguins.* And, Connor, that was an egg, not a turd."

"Whatever you say," Connor said with humor.

Aly tucked herself against Dylan's side and smiled up at him. "There's always next time."

He bent to kiss her cheek. "When you're here with me, losing still feels like winning."

She blushed and hugged his side tighter. It had taken Aly a little to get used to the idea of being a couple, but once she did she'd blossomed. Her entire demeanor had become softer, more approachable. Even Joanna had commented on it a few days earlier when he and Aly visited her farm. She said she'd never seen Aly look as happy or relaxed.

Just the night before, Aly had said something that had made Dylan's eyes mist up. She'd been talking about work. She said recently she was seeing a difference in how her patients were responding to her. They were smiling more, talking more openly with her. She hadn't made the connection that the difference was in her. He decided not to mention it in case it made her self-conscious.

With Aly, slow and easy won the race. She was letting her guard down with more and more people, smiling easier, taking offense less. She'd always been confident on a professional level, but her social circle hadn't extended much beyond Angelina and Joanna. He'd seen her at many Barrington events, but until recently he hadn't gotten the sense that she felt like she belonged.

Across the room, Dylan's father stood. "I have an early appointment tomorrow morning, so I'll be heading back early. As always, thank you, Sophie. Thank you, Dale."

Sean Sutton made his way around the room. When he approached where Dylan and Aly were, they both rose to their feet as well. He hugged Aly and said, "My son couldn't have chosen better. Will I see the two of you at my house next weekend?"

"Count on it." Smiling, Aly stepped back.

Dylan was next to give his father a back-slapping hug. "I'm going to teach her to catch and clean fish."

She laughed and rolled her eyes. "He is not."

Dylan amended his declaration. "I'm going to teach her to enjoy being on a boat while I fish, then hide while I clean them, but resurface to help cook."

Aly chuckled. "That I can do."

"Sounds like the deal I had with their mother," Sean said with none of the sadness that might have accompanied the statement a year ago. Dylan was glad to see his father was becoming more comfortable with talking about his wife. For too long he hadn't, thinking if he did it would upset his children. The opposite was true. Remembering her brought them comfort. "Dylan, do you have a minute? There's something I want to ask you before I go."

"In private" was implied and unexpected. Dylan glanced

at Aly. She nodded that he should go. "Sure."

They stepped out into the foyer and away from where people could hear. "You can tell me it's none of my business," his father said, "but have you met her father yet? You said you planned to."

"Not yet. She shuts down every time I mention it. I don't want to push for it before she's ready."

His father nodded. "I understand and I agree, but—"

"But?"

"But building a life with someone isn't just about the good times. That's the easy stuff. There will come a time when you'll reach a point where you can't continue to move forward until you face what she's afraid of—together."

Dylan sighed. He didn't like that he had the same sense. "I don't know if she's protecting me or herself from him. I tried to tell her that I'm not that sensitive. If he doesn't like me, he doesn't like me. It won't change how I feel about her."

His father took a moment before adding, "Navigating someone else's family is not an easy thing, but your mother did it well. She used to say her first priority was us, then our families. It meant my brother could be annoying and she would ignore it—for me. Her father could question my ability to support her and I would forgive him—for her. When my brother died, she wept with me, not because she loved him but because she loved me and she knew I wouldn't feel whole without him."

Dylan blinked a few times quickly. He didn't want to imagine his life without Connor. "I understand what you're saying."

"We all want to jump to the defense of the people we love, but when it comes to their family sometimes it's not that easy. When you finally meet her father, check your ego at the door and figure out what she needs from you—and that's what you give her."

After giving his father another tight hug, Dylan said, "I don't get the sense that her father is abusive. He didn't mistreat her. If he does I couldn't stand by and watch that, but I hear you. She loves him and she loves me. I won't make her feel she has to choose."

"I know you won't. And keep in mind that children often share traits with their parents. You said yourself Aly is slow to trust, slow to open up. Don't expect her father to be any different." He clapped a hand on Dylan's shoulder. "But I have no doubt that you will win him over. You have too much of your mother in you not to. In the end my family loved your mother, probably more than they did me."

After a short silence, Dylan said, "See you next weekend, Dad."

"I'm counting on it."

ON THE DRIVE back to her apartment later that evening, Aly didn't ask Dylan what his father had wanted to discuss with him in private. If it was important, she knew he'd tell her. She'd never been with a man who was as open and loving as he was. At first she'd fought a constant fear that it couldn't stay that way, but each day with him was better than the one before.

He approached every hurdle on the horizon with a positive attitude. Where would they live? He'd shrugged and said, "A house is just a house. We can have more than one."

"What about our careers?" she'd worried. "I'm planted where my clients are."

"Work is work. I'll take jobs that keep me in the US, and if that doesn't work we'll figure it out."

"I work a lot. Will it be too much for us?"

"I'm a grown man with shit I need to do as well. I also help run a community support program back in my hometown. We don't have to spend every moment together. When we can, we'll do things together. When we can't, it'll make the time we have together even sweeter. I wouldn't want to live in anyone's pocket."

"How would adding children work in this setup?"

"Are you pregnant?"

"No."

"Then we'll make the changes we need to when we get to that point. I'm earning enough from my movies that I won't always have to work. Or you might decide to focus on research more than taking patients. We won't know until we get there, but if we make the decisions together and with each other in mind, I'm confident it'll all work out."

Simple. Straightforward. With just a few words and a hug he could calm her down to her soul. This wasn't about tearing down her life so she could join his, it was about moving forward together. Situations that had seemed insurmountable suddenly were manageable because he valued her journey as well.

Just that morning, on a three-way video chat, Joanna and Angelina had asked her to describe what it was like to be with Dylan. She had struggled to boil down the wonder of it into just a few words. "I feel lighter. Happy. Hopeful. Better on so many levels."

Joanna's response had been, "Bradford said he thinks you're exactly what Dylan needed. Dylan was already redefining who he was, and you helped him find his footing again. He's right, Dylan looks more settled. And, like you, happier."

Aly reached out and took Dylan's hand in hers. He looked over with a smile and said, "I enjoyed tonight."

"Me too."

"Think you can handle it once or twice every month?"

"Absolutely." Especially since Joanna and Angelina would often be there as well. "The Barringtons are such a warm family. They made me feel welcome from the first day I met them."

"Same, even though Connor and I tested their patience a few times."

"Oh, my God, Kenzi showed me a video of a drunk volleyball game you all had in the pool in your underwear. She says you and your brother are the best thing that has ever happened to her family—well, outside of finding Kade."

Dylan raised Aly's hand to his lips and kissed it. "They were a little intense when we first met them, but it was understandable. And we were a little wild. Over time we just kind of met in the middle."

They obviously had. Ask any Barrington and they'd say

they were all much happier now too.

Like me.

From the outside Aly's life hadn't changed dramatically. She still went to her office five days a week. She still had time to work on her design teams and keep up on her reading. The difference was she didn't come home to an empty apartment anymore. Her messages weren't solely work related or from Joanna or Angelina. No, her life wasn't different, it was just fuller.

And her nights? She flushed as she relived some of those highlights in her mind. Everything Dylan was outside the bedroom—supportive, energetic, fun, sweet, confident—he was in it. She'd always enjoyed sex, but with him she'd found a new level of pleasure. She'd read clinical studies that claimed sex was more what happened in a person's mind than what was physically going on, but she hadn't believed it. She did now. Everything was different with Dylan. The simple act of holding hands became an incredibly sensual act when they exchanged a certain look. He could excite her more with a wiggle of an eyebrow than another man might with a box of sex toys. She'd given up trying to explain it and gave herself over to simply enjoying it.

"Viviana won't be at my dad's house next weekend. She and Grant will be out of town, but they asked if we wanted to go to dinner with them when they get back."

"I'd love that," Aly said, pulling herself back to the conversation at hand. "Your father is great. Does anything upset him?"

Dylan gave her hand a squeeze. "Not anymore. For a

while, after my mother died, everything seemed too much for him, but time passed and he came back around."

Aly inhaled audibly. "I wish I'd known my father before he lost my mother. I wonder if he was the same."

"Loss changes everyone." His fingers laced with hers. "I had a talk with my dad tonight . . . just before he left. He said something I think is worth sharing. I was looking at meeting your father in terms of me and how I would handle it. It's not about me, though. So, although I do think eventually you'll have to introduce me to him, I'm okay with waiting until you're ready. I can't say I understand what you're afraid will happen, but I can say I'll do my best to make sure I don't make it worse."

She covered her eyes with her free hand for a moment, then lowered it and came to a decision. "I love my father."

"I know you do."

"He won't approve of you. Not because of anything about you, but he has never approved of anyone I've been with."

With a small smile, Dylan said, "I'm pretty confident I'm nothing like the men you chose before me, but I'm going to love him because I love you."

She shook her head. "I don't know what he'll say to you, but it won't be nice." She closed her eyes briefly. "I can see exactly how it'll play out. He'll say something dismissive about you. I'll get angry and say something I don't mean. We'll argue. He'll say something he doesn't mean. I'll feel guilty about what he said to you, about what I said to him, and then in general just feel bad that I don't know how to fix the situation. Do you really want to put yourself through that?"

He sighed. "He's your father. He's part of you. You say he loves you. He'll come around."

"I wish I believed that. It's like there is a barrier between us. He's always been there for me, without ever letting me close." She looked out the window. "I've tried so many times, but nothing I've ever said has changed that."

He put a hand on her leg and gave it a supportive rub. "When I get discouraged about if someone likes me I ask myself WWCD—what would Connor do? Have you ever seen him around someone who doesn't like him? He doesn't believe it. He doesn't try to change their mind, but he also doesn't change for them. Eventually they give in and forget why they didn't like him in the first place. My father told me my mother was the same. I'm not as good at it, but it worked with you and me."

Her head snapped around so she could see his face. "There was never a time when I didn't like you."

He laughed. "Oh, the dagger looks and little verbal jabs you used to shoot at me said differently."

She chuckled and conceded. "Okay, so I wasn't always happy that I found you attractive and sometimes I might have been the teeniest bit jealous."

"See, and I could have taken it all personally, but I didn't. I knew that deep down you liked me, and you did."

She leaned over so her head was on his shoulder. "Thank God you didn't give up on me."

"Never."

"If you're really okay with meeting my father, I'll call him this week." She tried and failed to imagine a scenario where smiling and ignoring something her father said would make him like Dylan more.

He gave her thigh another supportive pat. "The good and the bad, Aly, that's what I'm signing up for. The good is the easy part. The tougher stuff . . . as long as we face it together there's nothing we can't do."

Never had she thought anyone could love her the way Dylan did—so completely. She wiped tears from the corners of her eyes and hugged his arm. "Are you being so sweet just so you'll get oral sex every night?"

He perked up at that. "Every night? Hell, I didn't even know that was an option. Sweet! You ain't seen nothing yet."

She laughed and shook her head. "It was a joke."

He brought a hand to his chest and made a dramatically sad face. "No, Doc, you don't joke about stuff like that. Fake winning lottery tickets and false promises of daily oral sex, those are two jokes no man will ever find funny." He sniffed. "It's the stuff dreams are made of."

Oh, Lord. She laughed.

He winked and joined in.

Chapter Eighteen

I N A SMALL town outside of New York City, Aly gripped the shoulder strap of her seat belt with both hands. Her intention was to release it, but she just sat there, staring straight ahead, attempting to calm her nerves.

"Your father's house is beautiful. Very different than I imagined. Is it historic?"

Breathe. In. Out. It's just a visit. Doesn't even have to be that long. "It is and because of it there's always something being repaired in it."

"With all those vines, the Gothic windows and the Tudor-style chimneys it looks like something straight out of a fairy tale."

"Yeah, everyone is surprised when they see where my father lives. Don't let anything about the house lead you to believe he has a softer side to him. He doesn't."

They both got out of the car. Dylan came around to meet her on her side. "Not even the stream with a bench and roses?"

Aly didn't bother to look in the direction of the garden. She'd grown up with it as a backdrop to her childhood. It was a place she could look, but not touch. "My father hates flowers. He pays a gardener to keep up the property, but you'll never see him outside enjoying it."

Dylan looked around. "There's a big yard. Did you have a playground?"

She shook her head. "No." She didn't want to think about the past. With more than enough wrong with the present, there was no need to go digging up old issues. "Let's just go in."

He laced his hand with hers and leaned down to kiss her ever so briefly on the lips. "It'll be okay, Aly."

"It will be," she said more forcefully than she meant to. "I'm sorry. I don't want to do this. You and I are so happy. I don't want to hear him tell me why we shouldn't be." Her eyes filled with tears. "Let's go. We can come back some other time."

He pulled her to his chest and held her for a moment. She hated the panic rising in her, and was disgusted by her weakness. "What do you think your father wants?" Dylan asked.

"I have no idea. All I know is I've never been it." Her entire body began to tremble. "Nothing I ever did was good enough to praise. No cut ever deep enough for him to comfort me. I say he loves me, but I really don't know that he does. Especially after spending time with your father and seeing how Dale is with his kids, I don't want to go in there and show you what I grew up with."

Dylan ducked his head down so he was eye level with her. "Aly, if he ever hurt you, we don't ever have to see him—ever. You have nothing you need to prove to me. I love you. All of you. Everything that you love about yourself and everything you don't. Tell me what you need and that's what we'll do."

His strength washed over her, calming her panic. She took one deep breath, then another. "He didn't hurt me, not the way you're thinking. If you asked him he'd probably say the only reason we don't get on is me. I've always had unrealistic expectations of what a family should be."

Dylan shook his head. "Viviana would handle this so much better, but I can almost hear what she'd say. You have a right to your feelings. He has a right to his. Both are equally valid. If you want to work things out you need to look at things through his eyes, not yours."

She looked over at the house and snippets from years of disagreements echoed in her mind. "I'll tell you what he wants—to judge. That's all he does. If you push for more, he pulls away."

"I met someone like that once."

Aly frowned. "I'm nothing like him." She shuddered. "Oh, my God, and if I am, don't have children with me. I—"

"Stop," Dylan said firmly. "Stop. I am not telling you that you won't make a good parent. I'm saying maybe your father is afraid of something. When you're afraid, you get defensive and sometimes a little snippy. Let's be honest. What if we went in there and let him do both but didn't hold it against him?"

"You're suggesting we let him say whatever he wants to

without reacting to it? His comments can be cutting."

"Words don't scare me. I may be wrong. Maybe after five minutes in there I'll concede that you're right and we'll both run for the car. Or maybe we'll Conner-fy him."

That brought a small smile to her lips. "Conner-fy?"

"We'll just sit there, being ourselves, liking him until he breaks down and starts liking us back."

Aly released some of her nervousness with a laugh. "I can't picture that working." She searched Dylan's face and her heart began to lighten. What was the worst thing that could happen in there with her father? A repeat of every disappointing conversation they'd had in the past? Dylan would be at her side if it happened and still be at her side when they left. That alone would make it different. "Okay, let's do this."

"If things get dicey, imagine him as a scared little hamster. Hammy was a biter before we came to an understanding."

"Hammy?"

On the way to the door of her father's home, Dylan told her about the hamster Viviana had bought him, hoping to teach him empathy. When her father opened the front door, Aly smiled at him in a way she never had before. For the first time, she put aside her fear that he didn't love her the way she loved him—and saw him as a terrified little hamster with a propensity to bite when cornered. "Hi, Dad. I'd like you to meet Dylan Sutton, the man I intend to marry."

Her father frowned. "I wasn't aware you were engaged."

She smiled up at Dylan. "We're not yet, but I'm all in

and so is he."

Dylan placed one hand on her lower back and held his other hand out toward her father. "Yes, I am. It's a pleasure to meet you, sir."

Her father looked them both over, chose not to shake Dylan's hand, and said, "We'll see, won't we? Come in."

Aly glanced up at Dylan to see how he was handling the less than warm welcome. He bent near her ear and whispered, "He's a bitey little sucker, but many hamsters are before you win them over."

The rising anxiety in her ebbed away. "I love you."

"I know. I know. We can explore that topic more later." He gave her a little nudge. "Right now I need to focus on leaving with all the fingers I came with."

She chuckled, an action that caused her father to halt and look over his shoulder at them. He did not look happy with either of them. Not nearly as intimidating, though, now that she was imagining him glaring up at her from a little cage. She smiled at her father. His frown deepened and he began walking again toward the library.

Of course he'd chosen that room. It was two stories of shelves filled with a mixture of the classics and medical journals, current and ancient alike. If the entire internet disappeared, she was pretty certain the bulk of human knowledge would be preserved as long as her father's library survived. Taking Dylan there was a blatant intimidation move. Her father didn't enter an encounter unarmed. He would have learned all he could about Dylan ahead of time. How long would it take him to bring up that Dylan hadn't attended college? Five minutes?

Once inside the library, her father said, "Take a seat."

There was no option of Dylan and Aly sitting together since all the chairs were meant for one, but Dylan chose one. None of the antique furniture in her father's house was meant for someone of Dylan's size and she prayed the chair didn't collapse beneath him. She chose a chair beside him. Her father remained standing.

"So, Dylan, you're from New York?"

"I am. Upstate."

"Where you worked in construction until your sister married one of the Barringtons."

"I'm flattered that you know so much about me," Dylan said.

"Don't be," her father answered in a tone that made Aly cringe. "It wasn't difficult to find out all about you. Your life is on display for all. I can't say I see what you and my daughter could possibly have in common."

"Dad," Aly said. "If you can't be civil this will be a very short visit."

Her father looked from her to Dylan and back. "Are you having some sort of breakdown? You're a little old for him to be an act of rebellion."

"I love him, Dad."

Her father looked Dylan over again. "If that's true, it's truly disappointing. I thought your taste was more refined."

Anger began to rise within Aly and a slew of defensive retorts came to mind. Without Dylan, she and her father would already be in a full-blown argument, no different than any other time she tried to discuss anything of importance with him. *Not this time, Hammy.* "If you take the time to get to know him, Dad, you'll see exactly why he's perfect for me. I tend to get all tangled up in my head and he has this beautiful way of calming the storm in me."

"A prescription is easy enough to obtain and it would be less likely to sleep with your friends."

Dylan gurgled. Aly looked at him and he quickly apologized with a wave of his hand. "I'm sorry. I didn't mean to laugh. That was a good one, though. I see where you get your sense of humor."

Folding his arms across his chest, Aly's father said, "You're making a mistake, Aly. He'll do nothing but drag you down. You're at the top of your career. If you push yourself, you might just make a difference. Is that what this is? Are you afraid of failing so you're choosing someone who will ensure you do?"

Aly rose to her feet. *Might make a difference?* This was the point where she would have normally started to feel shredded, but she didn't. *What does he want?* "Dad, Dylan and I are going to get married and have a herd of potentially unruly children, and we're going to bring them here. They'll probably drive you crazy, play in the stream, run through that garden—"

"No," her father barked. "No one goes in the garden."

Aly glanced quickly at Dylan. That fucking garden. It was a physical representation of her relationship with her father. How sad that even after all this time he would not only not let her in, but couldn't imagine admitting his future grandchildren either.

Dylan gave Aly a look of encouragement and made a little chomping move with his fingers. Aly took a deep breath then returned her attention to her father. *What is he so afraid of?* "Why, Dad? Why do you keep it up if you won't let anyone enjoy it?"

He turned away from her and looked out the window in the direction of the garden. "It's all I have left of your mother."

Aly swayed on her feet. Her father didn't talk about her mother—ever. She looked back at Dylan. He nodded for her to go to her father. Aly walked over to the window and stood beside him. "It's not, Dad. You have me. Even if you wish I'd died instead of her."

Her father stood absolutely still for what felt like an eternity, then seemed to deflate a little. "I've never wished that. I've wished you didn't share so many of the same features. I've hated that your laugh is so similar to hers that when I hear it I almost forget she's gone. I've wanted to forget and resented that with you I couldn't, but I never wished it was you instead." After a pause he said, "You don't have to keep me in your life, Aly. I stopped being the man she married the day she died."

Aly swallowed hard. "What was he like? The man my mother fell in love with?"

"Foolish." Her father's hands clenched at his sides. "He fell in love with a woman who believed in fairy tales and happy endings. She chose this house because she thought it would be the perfect place to raise our children. She planted that garden so our house would always be full of roses. And I bought into her fantasy. When we found out she was pregnant, it was validation that she was right and we could have the perfect life she envisioned for us."

"Then she left you."

"Yes." His tone was guttural and tortured.

It was the most real conversation they'd ever had and Aly was holding back tears, but just barely. Her father had held on to his pain as a way of holding on to his wife. "I'm so sorry." She hesitated, then just followed her heart and hugged him tightly. He didn't hug her back but she didn't let go. "I love you, Dad, and I'm not going anywhere. I want you at our wedding. I want you in my life. And our kids will come here, Dad, and they will play in that rose garden and if you don't like it . . ." She sniffed. "You'll have to suck it up because we're your family."

He looked down at her. The cold man who had raised her was gone. In his place was a much less confident father who looked tormented. "You always were a stubborn child." This time, his arm came around her in what was the first hug she could remember receiving from him.

She burst into tears. Any other time, she would have apologized for doing so, but she didn't. This was her. This was real. He needed to see her pain as well as his own.

He put his other arm around her and held her to his chest. Just held her while she cried.

ACROSS THE ROOM Dylan was misting up. *Holy fuck, if they don't knock it off soon I'll be bawling too.*

He stood quietly and left the room. The visit had started off rocky, but he was glad they'd come. Both Aly and her father had needed this. Hopefully now they could all move on—together.

Just outside the house, Dylan sat on the steps. He'd been waiting until he was sure Aly was ready before he proposed, but after how many times she'd said they were getting married asking her would be almost anticlimactic.

Unless he called in an expert. He took out his phone and texted: **I'm ready to ask Aly to marry me. Let the magic rain.**

Clay's response was a digital display of fireworks which Dylan took as a yes.

A few minutes later, Aly came outside and joined Dylan on the steps. Her eyes were red and puffy, but she looked a lot calmer than when they'd arrived. "I think my father is in shock. I've never cried in front of him and I pretty much just drenched the front of his shirt."

Dylan put his arm around her. "You both needed that."

"We did." She snuggled closer. "I think we're going to be okay now. I can't thank you enough. I couldn't have done it without you."

He kissed the top of her head. "You could have, but I'm glad I could be here with you."

"Me too."

"It was incredibly sweet of me."

"Yes, it was." She tipped her head back to meet his gaze. "Where are you going with this?"

He playfully kept his eyes wide and full of mock innocence. "Nowhere, just remembering how much you like it when I'm sweet and highlighting that this was a whole new level of it."

She laughed. "That's what's on your mind?"

He grinned. "Always. In fact, you never need to ask or ask permission. Just assume the answer is always yes." Then he kissed her smiling lips. It wasn't easy to turn off the heat once it started to rise in him, but he did. They not only had the night to look forward to, but all the nights after that. Meeting her father had reminded him of what he'd learned young: tomorrow was never guaranteed. All a person could do was love as hard as they could and savor every moment.

With one hand caressing his cheek, she said, "My father would like us to come back in."

Dylan rose to his feet and helped her to hers. "I'm proud of you, Aly. You faced your fears and his as well."

"Thank you." She tugged on his hand. "But stop or I'm going to cry again."

Her father met them at the door again. This time he held out his hand to Dylan. Without hesitation, Dylan took it and gave it a hardy shake.

As the door closed behind them, and they made their way through the house . . . this time to the living room, Dylan asked, "When can I start calling you Dad?"

Her father's mouth thinned.

Dylan kept his smile bright. "I'll give you some time to get used to the idea."

Chapter Nineteen

A COUPLE WEEKS later, while Dylan slept Aly called Clay early in the morning. "Is everything ready? Did everyone arrive?"

"I still feel like this is a conflict of interest, considering Dylan is my primary charge, but if you're determined to ruin your own surprise I can't stop you."

"Clay, Dylan has been so good to me. I want to make this special for him."

"I'm pretty sure you'll do that simply by saying yes."

She sighed. "You know what I mean. He does so much for others, I want him to see how many people care about him. You invited all of his friends from his hometown?"

"And flew them out."

She nodded. "And his friends from his last movie?"

"All of them as well."

"All the Barringtons?"

"Every damn one of them. And I swore them all to secrecy." In a kinder tone, Clay said, "Lexi wants you to know that she thinks this is the most romantic thing she's ever helped arrange."

"My father said he'll be there as well."

"I double-checked that he will." Clay coughed. "He's an acquired taste, isn't he?"

That was a kind way of putting it. "He is. Thank you, Clay. This means so much to me."

"Three for three. My matchmaking record is solid."

Aly could have questioned if it was really Clay who had gotten them together, but he'd done so much to make the proposal special for Dylan that she didn't mind giving Clay the credit for it all. "Someday I hope I can help you with something."

"No, need. I'm good."

He wasn't, but that was a conversation for another time. Aly needed to sneak back in bed and pretend she didn't know what Dylan had planned that day. "Thanks again, Clay. See you later."

Sex that morning was so tender Aly nearly wept after she came. She'd found him—her other half. Today they'd take another step toward making vows to each other, but she was already his in every way that mattered. *And he's mine.*

"What are you smiling about?" he murmured when he caught her looking at him.

"Just wondering if you know how wonderful you are."

He tipped his head to the side. "Are you being so sweet just so I'll go down on you every night? Because that is absolutely still on the menu even if you return to being a little snippy."

She did her best to mimic the expression he'd given her when she'd joked about daily oral sex. She brought a hand to her bare chest. "I sure hope you're not joking. That's the stuff dreams are made of."

He rolled over, opened a drawer, and returned with a small box. "Aly. I was going to do this later, but—"

She sat straight up. "No, don't ask me."

Holding the ring box in one hand he looked around. "Ooookay. You're not ready yet. I thought you were, but I can wait."

She turned so she was sitting cross-legged and naked next to him. "I'm ready for the question, but you're not allowed to ask me here." She made a pained face. "I want it to be special for you."

He moved to sit facing her. "I did have something more elaborate planned. Clay helped me arrange it. It has lots of flowers, musicians, some fireworks. Also, I think a gondola he flew in from Italy. I'm not really sure how that's going to work, but there's a pond at the park I chose . . . so maybe there?"

"I spoke to Clay as well."

He frowned. "Did he tell you what I planned? I went back and forth between asking you in private or inviting all your friends. I know you don't really like to be the center of attention so I figured I'd ask you here and we can celebrate there with everyone."

Never, never could she possibly love anyone more than she loved the man before her. "Clay didn't tell me everything, but he had to tell me some because I asked him to help me make the day special for you as well."

His face lit up. "You did?"

"I did. Should I tell you how or would you like to be surprised?"

"Tell me." After she did, he looked down at the box still in his hand. His eyes were shining with emotion. "I love you so much, Aly. I don't care if you say yes here or in front of everyone we know. As long as the answer is yes."

She took the ring box from him and opened it. It was a beautiful, delicate diamond ring. Simple. Classically romantic. She slipped the ring on her hand. It fit perfectly. "I do want to celebrate with everyone we love, but I'm wondering if you could ask me to marry you while we're both coming." She gave him a heated look. "Unless you think that would be too difficult to coordinate."

He went up on his knees and hovered his mouth just above hers. "Family and friends can wait, it's important for couples to have shared goals."

She laughed and rolled onto her back. "Yes, it is."

Rather than immediately joining her he spread her legs and settled himself between them, parting her sex with his fingers. "It might take a little practice to get our timing right. Are you okay with saying yes more than once?"

He slid a finger into her wet sex and twirled it deeply until he found that spot that always sent her wild. She jutted her hips against his hand. "If you insist," she said attempting to sound reluctant, then gasped as he bent and began to circle her clit with that strong tongue of his. "Ask as many times as you want."

He chuckled against her sex and thrust a second finger into her. "Then if you'd like, you can ask me."

She couldn't imagine a better way to propose. It took them hours to get their timing perfect, but they were both glowing when they finally headed off to the park to celebrate their engagement with friends, family, fireworks, and a gondola.

THE END

Not ready to say good-bye to these characters? Sign up for my newsletter via my website ruthcardello.com/newsletter and stay informed about releases.

To get a complete list of all my books to to:
www.Ruthcardello.com

About the Author

Ruth Cardello was born the youngest of 11 children in a small city in southern Massachusetts. She spent her young adult years moving as far away as she could from her large extended family. She lived in Boston, Paris, Orlando, New York—then came full circle and moved back to New England. She now happily lives one town over from the one she was born in. For her, family trumped the warmer weather and international scene.

She was an educator for 20 years, the last 11 as a kindergarten teacher. When her school district began cutting jobs, Ruth turned a serious eye toward her second love – writing – and has never been happier. When she's not writing, you can find her chasing her children around her small farm, riding her horses, or connecting with her readers online.

Contact Ruth:
Website: RuthCardello.com
Email: Ruthcardello@gmail.com
FaceBook: Author Ruth Cardello
Twitter: @RuthieCardello

Printed in Great Britain
by Amazon

45912896R00145